PRAISE FOR
Second Time's a Charm

"Mary Flinn is the female equivalent of author Nicholas Sparks. Her characters are as real as sunburn after a long day at the beach. Hot days and hotter nights make *Second Time's a Charm* an excellent sultry romance that will stay with readers long after the sun goes down. The second book in a trilogy, this story is a movie waiting to happen."

~Laura S. Wharton, author of
The Pirate's Bastard and Leaving Lukens

"*Second Time's a Charm* is a charm to read. Mary Flinn knows how to make the everyday world real as her words cast a spell over the reader, a spell that only ends all too soon…. I almost felt ready to go out and buy a wedding present and try to decide what to wear to the ceremony because after all, the characters of Tyson and Stacie had become my good friends and I expected to dance at their wedding."

~Tyler R. Tichelaar, Ph.D. and author of
the award-winning *Narrow Lives*

"Set on North Carolina's Outer Banks, *Second Time's a Charm* is a grown-up story of forgiveness and redemption, as forty-year old Stacie Edmonds and thirty-year old Tyson Garrett take the plunge into the uncharted waters of taking a second chance on love. A steamy departure from Mary Flinn's previous young adult romance, *The One*, this story and these characters, both new and familiar, are sure to seduce the reader. The only disappointment is that it has to end!"

~Patrick Snow, International Best-Selling Author of
Creating Your Own Destiny and *The Affluent Entrepreneur*

"What a GREAT read by Mary Flinn! I so enjoyed *The One*, her first novel, and I think *Second Time's a Charm* is fantastic! As a restaurant owner and a resident of the Outer Banks of North Carolina, the story captured me and drew me close—right to the very end. Mary Flinn nailed it! I look forward to her next book."

**~Carole Sykes, owner of Sam and
Omie's Restaurant, Nags Head, NC**

Second Time's a
Charm

A Novel

Fiction Worx

Mary Flinn

DEDICATION

Dedicated to my husband, Mike, the love of my life,

whom I was lucky enough to find the first time around.

You keep it real, and fun!

ACKNOWLEDGMENTS

Many people continue to inspire and encourage me in the baring of my soul on the pages that follow.

Thanks to all of my family, the lights of my life, my young adult daughters in particular, of whom I am so proud, Jessica and Shelby.

Leslie Murphy, Denise Ballard, Suzanne Carlson, and Terri Jones inspired the characters of Murph, Bets, Sue, and Dr. Karen Walters with their wit, charm, and steadfast friendship. I will always laugh the most with you all!

Thanks to my extended families, the people who support and guide me, particularly my Saint Francis Episcopal Church friends and the staff at Jesse Wharton Elementary School.

Thanks especially to Mary Susan and her book club, with whom I enjoyed drinking wine, Lori, Amy, Laura S. Wharton, Terri Jones, Suzanne Woodard, and Laura Ambler all of whom took the time to read this manuscript and offer encouragement.

To the women of Sam and Omie's Restaurant in Nags Head, NC, Carole, Jakey, and Judy: I enjoyed reminiscing with you all about the good old days, The Sound Side, and that person we remember who started this journey into fiction for me! We'll do more reminiscing soon!

This book would not exist without the patient guidance of my editor and proofreader, Dr. Tyler Tichelaar, who through his endless kind, constructive criticism has led me out of my addiction to both adjectives and conjunctions into the better writer I aspire to be.

To Shiloh Schroeder, thank you for turning this book into the work of art it is.

Finally to Patrick Snow, much gratitude for your ever-present guidance and vision for carrying me to the next phase of my writing, the second book!

Contents

Chapter 1

THE SOUND SIDE

She wanted to meet him in the walk-in refrigerator. She stood beside him in the kitchen of her restaurant, arranging her homemade key lime pies to stow in the walk-in. She watched him out of the corner of her eye, as he placed the scoop of fresh tuna salad onto the bed of spring mix, garnishing it with grape tomatoes, cucumbers, and julienned carrots. Their hands touched from time to time as they worked on the line, sending a current of energy through her. Tyson Garrett was the sexiest man she had ever seen, with his surfer's tan and mop of dark curly hair that had probably never seen a comb, wearing a faded lime green T-shirt and khaki shorts under his white apron. She hoped her famous poker face was in place for the sake of her other employees who were milling about, cleaning up from lunch and prepping the kitchen for the dinner shift. Her nephew, Kyle, the last waiter to take out an order, waited at the kitchen line, tapping his thumb idly to the Doors' "Riders on the Storm" that played on the radio, and eyeing the French fries on a plate he had arranged on the tray.

"Don't even think about it, pal," Stacie said, grinning at him. She knew he'd be starving as he was the last to finish his shift and have his own lunch. He looked across at her with his blazing blue eyes, like hers, under sun streaked light brown bangs, flicking them out of his eyes, and grinned back at her.

"Uh, *sorry*, can't you hear my stomach growling? You don't feed me enough around here!"

Tyson was grinning, too, his deep set green eyes crinkling at the corners, dimples appearing on each side of his wide, white smile. "Got your lunch right here, dude. I've got your back, even if *she* doesn't," he said slowly, in his laid-back way, flashing his eyes at her, sending yet another wave of lust riveting through her body. It was dangerous being in love with her chef, especially when he was ten years her junior, and she kicked herself every day for letting her feelings get out of hand the way they had. It had never been her plan…but so far they had maintained the perfect balance of professionalism at work and romance in private. He had never been intimidated by her status as his boss, or the difference in their ages.

She spoke to Kyle then. "So when is Chelsea getting here?" His girlfriend was here, visiting for a while from their home in the mountains. He had been miserable without her when he and his mother had moved to Southern Shores, North Carolina just weeks before. They would be starting at separate colleges in the fall and the uncertainty of what lay ahead of them seemed to add to Kyle's distress. Stacie could read his moods vividly, after having formed a bond with him when he spent the previous summer at her home in nearby Duck while working as a dishwasher in her place.

His face lit up, noticeably. "Any time. We're going skim boarding again today at the beach."

"Wow, she's a glutton for punishment after busting her ass yesterday!" Tyson laughed.

Kyle nodded proudly, "Yeah, she's tough. She'll get the hang of it," he said, confidently, taking the tuna plate and heading out the swinging door to the dining room.

Stacie wiped her hands on her white apron and captured a stray blonde hair that had come loose from her messy bun; she turned to check on Nina at the computer screen, totaling up her last bill for her shift. Nina ran her fingers through her curly blonde hair, flipping it all over to one side. Her hair fell to just her collarbone, and the sight of that simple gesture sent a pang of loss through Stacie.

Nina had noticed and looked up from her bill. "You okay, Stace?" she asked, concern showing in her eyes.

Stacie wrapped her arm around Nina's shoulders and gave her a squeeze. "Yeah, sweetheart. Sometimes you just remind me of my niece, Desiree. I still really miss her," she said. Kyle's older sister had been killed in a tragic spring break accident about four years ago. Those moments hit her unexpectedly sometimes, making it impossible to conjure up the poker face at times.

Nina hugged her back and their heads touched for a moment. "I'm sorry," she said, wiping crumbs off her aqua T-shirt, proclaiming *The Sound Side Bar and Grill*, returning her ticket to the black folder, and following Kyle out the door.

Just then, a stunning-looking girl in a flowered tank top and a minute jean skirt, swimsuit straps exposed, appeared at the kitchen door. Her wavy, dark auburn hair was pulled back into a loose pony tail and her pale aquamarine eyes were striking in her sun-kissed face. She carried a striped canvas bag slung over one shoulder. Her legs were unbelievably slim and shapely and ended in worn leather flip-flops: a ballet dancer's legs.

Stacie's mood improved instantly and she smiled broadly. "Hi, Chelsea! You look great! Kyle's out in the dining room."

"Yes, I saw him. He was finishing with his table. I just came in to say hey. How are y'all?" she asked, smiling at Stacie and Tyson, who grinned back at her.

"Well, hey. We're good. How are *you* today?" asked Stacie, intending to inquire about the obvious bruises the girl must surely have from her trial with Kyle's skim board the day before.

She grimaced. "Good, but a little sore!"

"I'm sure you are!" Tyson laughed. "Good for you for getting back on the horse."

"Oh…I'll try anything!"

Kyle appeared in the doorway behind her and placed his hands at her waist, startling her so she jumped. "Hey! Want some lunch?" he asked, giving her a kiss on her cheek and going to the line to get his plate Tyson was sliding his way.

"No thanks. I ate a sandwich with your mom before I left. She's feeling a lot better today."

Everyone nodded. Shelly Davis had fallen and broken her ankle three weeks ago when they had moved into their new house in Southern Shores, and after surgery, her recovery had been painful and slow. "Have my grandparents gotten there yet?" Kyle asked Chelsea.

"Not yet. She said just your grandmother was coming today to help her out, and that your granddad would be getting here by the weekend, in time for the party."

Stacie waved her hand in the air and made a whooshing sound. "Don't remind me. Turning forty can take its time getting here."

Chelsea laughed, "Like you *really* look forty. You could pass for twenty-five any day of the week."

Stacie hugged her and laughed her deep throaty laugh. "This is why we keep you around. You're so good for my head!" Tyson winked at Stacie and wiped the counter, flipping off the food warmer lights in the process.

Zack, the bar manager, poked his head in the door at that moment. His large shoulders and imposing presence made them all turn and look. "Hey, Stacie, Reggie's here."

"Thanks, Zack. I'll be right there."

Tyson shot her a look before she followed Zack out. "I'm gonna start prepping the halibut for tonight's specials while you guys are going over the bar inventory."

"Okay, thanks. What are you going to do to it?" she asked, at the doorway.

He shrugged, "Almond crusted, pan-seared with a miso sauce, over polenta with roasted asparagus…how does that sound?"

She wilted, rolling her eyes back in her head. "My *favorite!*" she said, taking off her apron and hanging it on its peg by the door.

"You say that about all the food," he snickered.

"Hi, Reg," she greeted the alcohol distributer rep who had installed himself at the bar, already going over the week's inventory that Zack had produced for him.

"Hi, Stace," he said, rising and kissing her on the cheek. He was a sharp-looking man in his forties with cleanly cut and gelled brown hair. He wore a pair of gray slacks and a deep blue and white striped shirt she immediately liked. They got down to business, weighing out the liquor bottles and comparing them to the inventory sheets as he did at her request sometimes on Mondays. As she watched him, she exchanged nervous glances with Zack, who waited patiently in his black T-shirt with a graphic design eagle printed in bronze, highlighting the breadth of his wide chest. After a while, Reggie told her what she didn't want to hear. "Either someone's a lousy pour, or you've got somebody giving away drinks to their friends. Either way, they're stealing from you," he said seriously. "This is getting progressively worse every week. You want to consider using the measuring pour spouts?" She and Zack looked at each other again and Zack frowned at the idea. It wasn't his problem, or Andrew's. They were doing just fine all by themselves. Stacie shook her head. The discrepancy problem hadn't happened until this summer. Zack and Andrew had been her bartenders for a couple of years now, and she trusted their loyalty completely. Every so often with the summer help, the problem arose and then decreased as the new people's skills improved with practice. Kate was the new summer bartender, and having just turned twenty-one, she didn't have any experience. But after six weeks, she should be improving. Maybe they needed to do another training session with her. Stacie liked Kate and wanted to give her the benefit of the doubt.

"We should have a meeting after Kate's shift tonight," Stacie said and Zack nodded. "Let's run her through a practice pouring session again and see if she doesn't get the message."

Zack nodded, and then asked, "Do you want Andrew here too? I can call him…."

"That's a good idea. That way it doesn't look like I'm singling her out. Don't be mad at me. I won't be nice, but we know it's not you…or Andrew." She met Zack's eyes and he nodded. He fingered the touch screen on his phone, getting on the call to Andrew. After a while, she and Reggie had finished their business and she checked on Tyson in the kitchen.

"All right, everything looks good in here," he said to her. He had turned off the lights. "The specials are printed out for tonight and Nina will be putting them together for the tables when she gets back at four. And I'm…going surfing," he said with a slow smile and a hand around her waist. They were alone in the old weathered marina-turned-restaurant, so she lifted her chin to let him kiss her passionately, gently pressing her against the wall, and stroking the side of her throat. "Is there anything else you need me to do for you before I go?" he asked softly and suggestively.

She swallowed, attempting to appear more collected than she felt, and said, "Not at the moment. I'm sure I'll think of something later."

"Then, I'll be waiting to hear from you later," he said, giving her another short kiss and squeezing her hand before he released her and untied his apron. His green eyes sparkled at her and a smile played at the corner of his mouth. He was out the back door before she knew what was happening. As his truck growled to life, she slowly picked up her purse, locking the doors behind her.

Later that night, after the wait staff had left and the dishwashers finished up under Tyson's supervision, the three bartenders assembled at the bar, waiting for Stacie. In her office, she checked herself in the mirror, applying lip gloss and straightening her silky, turquoise sundress. She rubbed hand lotion into her hands, always dry from so much time in the kitchen. *Make them sweat a minute longer*, she thought. She let out a deep breath and walked out to meet them. Kate, incredibly tanned, in a black tube top and French manicured nails, attractive with her straight blonde hair pulled tightly back in the usual pony tail, looked decidedly worried, her hands clasped tightly on top of the bar in front of her. Usually she conveyed an air of confidence and displayed her bright white teeth in a large smile that set off her ice blue eyes under dark brows. This evening, she just looked scared to death. Stacie smiled at her encouragingly, and then brought it up short.

She ran her hand through her long blonde hair, sighed sharply, and said, "Okay, guys, there's no easy way to say this. Somebody's going to get fired if some things don't change around here." She looked pointedly at Zack, and then at Andrew, stunningly handsome in his own right, and then at Kate, whose face went pale. They were her sexual trifecta, and had attracted both women and men from up and down the beach into her establishment. "One of you is stealing me blind in the liquor department. I don't know who it is, but we need to settle this tonight or one of you is gone." Andrew's heavy dark brows were knit in concern, and Zack was stoic on his end. Kate glanced nervously from one to the other of them and then back at Stacie. "There's one of two things going on; either somebody still can't pour, or one of you is giving away freebies, and that's a big no-no around here." She looked at them each again; Kate was twisting her pearl earring, glancing at the guys. Andrew shot Kate a look, but Zack ignored her completely. "So do you think we need a little wrist-popping review? Anybody? What about you, Kate?" Stacie asked, more gently. "I know you're new at this. Zack's a really good teacher," she said and inclined her head for him to move around behind the bar.

Kate's face flamed, but she shrugged, looking to Andrew for support. Zack took his place and lined up five shot glasses as Stacie pulled out a fifth of vodka for the practice. He poured vodka into each glass, popping his wrist at precisely the right time, coming up with a perfect ounce in each glass. "Nicely done!" laughed Stacie, pouring the vodka into a pitcher and motioning Kate to come back and try her hand.

As she held the bottle, Kate's hand shook noticeably; she poured the first shot, spilling vodka over the top, and sucked in her breath in frustration. "Here," said Zack, demonstrating again. "Snap it quick, right before you think you need to." When she did it again into the next glass, with less spillage this time, Andrew clapped for her. "All right! Do it again," Zack said. She snapped her wrist again, this time with no spill but not a complete shot. "Good. Try it again, but don't be quite so short," said Zack. She poured the next one perfectly. Stacie and Andrew both applauded her then, and Stacie put an arm around her.

"That's great, Kate. Do ten more," she said and lined up some more shot glasses, pouring the vodka back into the pitcher, which would soon be returned to the bottle. She watched absently as Kate pressed her lips together and began pouring under Zack's direction and Andrew's rapt attention. Stacie took her phone from her purse and called Tyson.

She wandered away from the group, back to her office, and spoke to him softly in the phone. "We're about to wrap this up. Are you home?"

"Waitin' on you, babe," he said lazily. She could hear the smile in his voice.

Her house was mostly dark when she arrived, except for a night light in the kitchen. He had turned on his favorite music. Van Morrison was singing about what a marvelous night it was for a "Moondance." She thought he had lit a candle in the bedroom, but then realized it was the moon. It wasn't full yet, but the night was clear and it was as bright as a beacon through her windows. He sauntered out from the kitchen to greet her, handing her a glass of chilled white wine, his eyes glittering at her in the dark. She ran a hand through her hair and felt the tension from the night melt away as she sipped the cool, fruity pinot. This moment was exactly what she needed, and he knew it. He was exactly what she needed. He clinked his glass against hers.

"So, did you kill anybody tonight?" he asked, humoring her.

A laugh bubbled up from inside her as she looked at him appreciatively. "Nope. They're all alive…and employed, still. Zack is a really good actor! And Andrew too, I guess. I don't know what Zack told him."

"I take it you scared Kate to death?"

"Well, I don't think she had any idea to what extent we can track the bar inventory. I think she'll be on her best behavior now. I hate to do that, but it's just the best way to get someone's attention."

He chuckled. "You're really good at what you do."

"Just protecting my interests. I really don't like firing people."

"Everybody loves you, boss," he said, setting his glass down and taking hers, setting it down too, sliding his arms around her waist, flooding her with warmth, melting her further.

"Don't start this *boss* shit with me tonight," she warned.

"Well, then, how about this? Everybody loves you, *Stacie*…especially me," he said, pulling her hips close to his and kissing her mouth tenderly, over and over. She slid her hand up the side of his neck, caressing him, kissing his throat, her fingertips ending in the soft dark curls of his hair.

Instantly, he recognized her intent and said hopefully, "Tonight?"

She nodded. It had been over two weeks since they'd made love and she was saving the surprise for just this moment. She had the longest periods of any woman she knew. Her doctor had taken care of this and then that, but she still had problems. Childbearing at her age was looking more and more doubtful, to her dismay—and Tyson's, she learned after sharing their dreams for the future. But they did not talk about this much. She looked deep into his eyes and he held her again, his hands in her hair, breathing in her perfume, and moaning that he wanted her, softly in her ear. It had seemed like forever since they had been close the way they wanted. She murmured into his ear, "God, you're the most patient man in the world." She pressed her mouth into his neck and kissed him.

He led her into the bedroom where they stood in front of the window, hearing the ocean roll and crash just beyond the boardwalk, as the warm breeze blew over them, fluttering the curtains. Moonlight flooded the room as he kissed her again, parting her lips, and she tasted the wine they'd shared. He touched her face with his fingertips and traced them back, behind her ear, to her neck, until he rested his other hand over her heart. With both palms, she pulled his face into hers and kissed him passionately. She kissed the cleft in his chin, feeling the stubble on her lips that he would shave in the morning. Slowly, she unbuttoned his shirt and peeled it off of him, her hands moving across the smooth skin of his shoulders, his chest, and the flatness of his stomach. She undid the button of his jeans and pushed her hands inside. He groaned, his hands moving up and down her back, sensually. He found the zipper on her dress and slid it down, moving the straps over her shoulders, her dress slipping to the floor in a soft blue puddle. Kissing her gently, he eased her back onto the bed so he could lie beside her, caressing her skin, his touch sending her arching off the bed, as the balmy breeze blew over them. He was so tender with her, and he touched her so intuitively she could hardly catch her breath, giving herself to him in return. It had never been like this with her husband, even from the beginning. She ached to please this beautiful man, and at the same time, she wanted to take all of him. No matter how hard they pressed themselves into each other, it was as if they couldn't get close enough. Waves of passion poured through them over and over as they moaned and breathed the language of love into each other's ears.

Later, as they lay entwined with each other, kissing and touching, he traced his fingertips down the side of her face and sought her eyes again. He laid the palm of his hand over her breast, feeling her heartbeat, and she covered it with her own. She could see his eyes, deep and sparkling in the moonlight, penetrating hers with intensity just before he spoke. "Why won't you marry me?" he asked her.

She sighed. "It doesn't take a ring on my finger to show you how much I love you. Everybody we know can see it," she said, placing the palm of her hand tenderly on his face and touching his lips with her thumb. "Marriage wouldn't change the way I feel about you."

"I know you've been burned before, with your divorce. I have too, in my own way. But I want us always to be together. I want you to have my baby," he whispered.

She smiled ruefully. "You know that's what I've always wanted. But there's a chance it might not happen, at least not for me. If it's what you want, you should have the chance. I know what it's like to have that chance taken away from you. It wouldn't be fair…and you would regret it. I can't hurt you like that. Besides, you could meet someone younger than me… younger than you, even. I want you to be able to walk away if I'm not what you want…later."

"Are you kidding me? You're what I've always wanted. I'm not walking away. Babies or no babies, it's us I want."

"I know you would feel weird about living in my house, but it would be fine with me if you wanted to move in."

"I'd feel like such a dick living in your house, but I'm ready to be with you."

"I know you like having your own space. I know you surfer types!" she laughed quietly, stroking his well-muscled arm and shoulder, her hand resting on the warm knoll of his chest. "Isn't this every man's dream? No strings, great sex, the best kind of love there is?"

"Don't do this," he whispered. His eyes flashed at her and he held her gaze. "You *know* what I want. You just say the word…I'm yours."

Chapter 2

AGE MATTERS

Stacie pulled into the bank parking lot as the sun seared down on her head and shoulders inside the white convertible Volkswagen Cabrio she drove. She picked up the deposit bag she needed to drop off, slung her yellow purse over her shoulder, and shook out the eyelet blouse she wore that was damp from the short drive over. She would meet Kyle and Chelsea at the beach near her house later, and she was glad that her mother was in town again to take care of her sister Shelly, keeping her company while they all took a respite. Shelly, used to being fiercely independent and vain about her well-maintained appearance, had not handled her broken ankle and her resulting limitations very well. Surely, Mom's humor and creativity would be helpful, and Mom had been dying to get back to the beach, to help cook, unpack, and decorate the new little house. Kyle and Chelsea needed a respite as much as anybody, Stacie knew. After a tough senior year, heaped with mishaps and personal tragedy, not to mention the normal pressures from academics and other involvements, they were ready to have some fun, and just chill. Stacie could handle some chill, herself.

As she entered the cool, dimly lit bank, she slid her sunglasses on top of her head and wiped perspiration off the back of her neck with the palm of her hand. This summer was a scorcher already, and some major storms were probably in store for later. She felt the air conditioning swoosh pleasantly under her skirt as she stood in the long line, typical after lunch on a Friday. Absently, she glanced around, looking at the pictures on the walls, old photographs of the Wright brothers' first plane, the large dunes, known as Jockey's Ridge, and the famous Outer Banks ponies. She was vaguely aware that others had joined the queue behind her, and she smelled him before she saw him. Her ex-husband, Rick Boutwell, had always gone too heavy for her taste on the cologne, and he apparently wore the same ostentatious scent for his new wife that had repulsed her at the end of their marriage. It must have been what *she* liked. She sighed, soundlessly, closing her eyes so she could roll them in private. She hoped he would not make a scene, here in the bank where people knew them. It was hard to avoid him on the island, but at least with them both being in the restaurant business, she could ensconce herself in her own place and escape as much as possible.

Typically for him, he was doing his best to make her feel uncomfortable, even as she prayed for discretion on his part. She felt him inching closer to her until his breath was on her neck as he spoke her name in greeting. She did not jump, as he had probably intended her to do, but said his name blandly in response. "Rick. What's up?"

"Just hangin' out at the bank with the ex-old lady," he chuckled. "What's up with you? How's your business?"

"Really good, actually," she said and it was true. She felt more exhausted than she did most summers. Maybe it was because she slept so little, as a result of all the wild love-making she'd been doing lately. The thought made her smile, and she turned around to see whether he was gloating as usual. He looked strangely interested. His eyes roved over her and lingered too long at the neckline of her blouse.

"We've been pretty busy, too," he said. "There are a lot of people down already. The Fourth should be a killer. So, you're still with Tyson?" he asked, fishing. He was handsome in his dark-haired, well-dressed magazine spread look, but the effect had been lost on her for years now.

"Yes," she said, knowing he was going somewhere with this.

He was nodding absently. "You look really good, Stace. You've lost weight."

"How are Torie and the baby?" she deflected, realizing too late that she had allowed more ice to show in her eyes than she had intended, and he had seen it.

His brown eyes shone at her with something she couldn't quite figure out. "Everybody's good; keepin' me hoppin'…so you have the big day coming up, huh? The big *four-oh*? That makes Tyson, what, ten years younger…or more?"

"*Oh*…are you looking for new members in your *robbing-the-cradle club*?" she asked, laughing her throaty laugh. He had robbed the cradle himself when he had cheated on her a few years ago with Torie, who had been twenty-two to his thirty-something at the time. He had been the big partier, the hot shot entrepreneur, the one *never* to want children, but lo and behold, after two years together, she had gotten pregnant and they had held the coolest of beach weddings. It had been the social event of the island last summer, although, Stacie, of course had not attended.

His eyes narrowed slightly at her. "Nice. So is he living with you now? Come on, the guy *works* for you. Isn't that weird?"

"He works *with* me. And, no, he doesn't live with me. He's the best chef on the beach and he runs an orderly kitchen…no cussing, no screaming."

"But he *surfs*, right? I guess the cougar thing could work for you too," he said.

It was her turn to step to the counter, and her friend Sharon, the teller, was inclining her head toward her, saying, "Next?"

She had mulled over and over just what to say in such a situation, during fitful nights when she couldn't sleep, wishing for just this opportunity. And then, in her hoarse, sexy voice that men seemed to like, it came flying out of her mouth before she could even think about it, "Since when does age correlate with manhood? Tyson's *twice* the man you ever thought about being."

His eyebrows cranked up a notch, but he made no response as she stepped to the counter, greeting Sharon, who was chuckling discreetly.

Chelsea's skim boarding skills had improved dramatically since Stacie had watched her a few days ago. Stacie, relaxed in her beach chair, rubbed sunscreen into the hot skin of her arms as Tyson approached, carrying a beach towel and a Frisbee.

"Whoa! Look at her go!" he said, his dimples appearing, admiring Chelsea's new skills and sitting down beside Stacie. He glanced over at her and growled into her ear, "You look *amazing*. Wearing my favorite bikini, I see. Want me to do your back?" he asked, hungrily. She turned to let him massage the lotion into her skin. "You look like one of those Ralph Lauren models with that tousled blonde hair and enormous blue eyes… it's enough to make a guy melt."

"Keep it up and we might have to *leave* shortly," she said, making him laugh. The skim boarders were walking toward them, bodies wet and shiny, and smiling, out of breath. "You're doing *great*!" Stacie complimented Chelsea, handing her a towel.

"Thanks! It's really fun when you're not falling on your butt half the time," Chelsea said, grinning at Kyle.

Stacie was amazed at the changes she saw in her handsome nephew. Physically, he had bulked up after a successful football season in high school, and he was still working out, preparing to play football on a scholarship to Virginia in the fall. Stacie didn't know much about their team, but she knew he was pursuing their highly ranked architectural program, on an academic scholarship no less. She could not have been prouder of him if he were her own son. More significantly, he had matured remarkably since he had come to her last summer, to wash dishes in her restaurant, arrogant and angry, after the suicide of his father months before. He had grown up as a child of privilege, with no idea how to talk about his feelings or express his humility, anger, and angst. Shelly had tried to protect him from all the ugliness, first about the death of his sister three years before, and then from the circumstances leading to her husband's depression and suicide. It had not helped Kyle, but instead had driven a wedge between the two of them. Tyson had helped Stacie try to break through the stone façade Kyle had built around himself, and he was now starting to make progress taking it down. But it had taken meeting Chelsea to heal him, and to enable him to reinvent himself as the person she made him want to be. They were the loves of each others' lives, their touchstones. Stacie felt a pang of poignancy sweep through her heart, trying to imagine finding that kind of love at such a young age. It had taken her almost forty years. She watched them arranging themselves on beach towels next to her. Their eyes would meet, their hands would touch, and the feelings between them were palpable. Even Tyson was noticing, and he glanced at her, raising his eyebrows. It would be a short afternoon at the beach for all of them.

The sky had just turned the deep horizon blue of evening that Sunday night as The Sound Side's parking lot became packed with her birthday party guests' cars. It was no use trying to surprise Stacie Edmonds about her party. She was more intuitive than any of them, and no one lived in a place large enough to accommodate the crowd. If she were being led to the marina on their day off, under the guise of anything but work, she would be sure to know that something was up. At least they had told her to come later so she could walk in and see the crowd in place. The effect was not lost on her as her knees became a little weak and the butterflies flew around inside her, in anticipation of the event. She had dressed in a filmy, midnight blue dress with braided straps that hugged her figure attractively. She wore the pale blue sea glass earrings that Tyson had bought her on their trip to the Caymans that January. The silver bracelet on her wrist caught the full moonlight as she stepped onto the restaurant's walkway, examining it as if she were a first time visitor. The old, weathered siding with its ancient shutters propped open and the wide porch were reminiscent of earlier times when life on the island was more severe, and wild and remote. The red and green boat lights near the door, and the faint clanging of sea buoys in the sound beyond, added to the mystique of the place, along with the soothing lapping of water at the dock. She could hear the frogs and cicadas adding their music to the night. The warm breeze was damp and smelled of the sea, and she pulled her hair away from her face as she stepped inside the door.

Andrew was the first person at the bar to greet her as she made her entrance. He was breathtaking, as usual. He carried his tall and lanky frame serenely, and his thick, dark brown hair was fingered back from his face, in which sultry gray eyes looked out from under thick dark brows. His slow, boyish smile crept across his face when he saw her, transforming his brooding look to sunshine in just an instant. That transformation was what the women on the beach were always talking about.

"Hey, you're here!" he said, coming around the bar and taking her hand, kissing it gallantly. "Happy birthday!"

She began to relax and hugged him, thanking him and letting him escort her into the dining room where all of her friends and family were sharing laughs and drinks, waiting for her, with music playing. Tyson was standing by the kitchen with the Mary Washington college students, a group of girls, including Kate, who had worked there as waitresses over the last two summers. He was crumpling a large paper banner that proclaimed, *Lordy, lordy, Stacie's forty.* "Now, we said none of that, remember?" he laughed, tossing the paper into a trash can inside the kitchen door. When she caught his eye, he smiled immediately, going to her and taking her hand from Andrew. He wrapped an arm around her waist and kissed the side of her face and then her lips, saying low into her ear, "Happy Birthday! You look *fantastic!*"

As people began to notice her, a crowd of well-wishers circled around her. Kyle and Chelsea were there, giving her hugs. Her mother and father, Dan and Elaine Edmonds, had brought Shelly, who was installed at a picnic table on the large deck, where most of the others had congregated. Shelly had commanded a good bit of attention, with her cast, and the accompanying story. Her father, large and gray-haired, and so handsome in the latest new eyeglasses and short-sleeved seersucker shirt tucked into khaki pants, made his way to her and wrapped her into his familiar bear hug. "There you are! My understated and elegant girl! Happy birthday to you, my dear!"

Her mother was behind him, covered in abalone shell jewelry, wearing sharp white linen pants, bejeweled sandals, and a crisp pink blouse that set off her short, silver-blonde hair. "Darling, you look *wonderful!* Happy birthday! They say forty is the new thirty, but you look about *twenty*, sweetheart! Look how thin you are!" Stacie laughed and went to Shelly, who couldn't get up, to get a hug from her older sister as well. She was lovely as always, slim and perfect-looking, in her silvery green sundress, dripping in diamonds. Her friends, Rob and Jeanna, realtors with whom Shelly would be working once her ankle healed, wished her happy birthday and squeezed her hands. Stacie walked out onto the deck with Tyson, greeting the Duck ladies from their "book club," Murph, Bets, and Sue, and their husbands who stood in a group, discussing their summer home improvement projects. The women greeted her enthusiastically and took her in a group hug, laughing about their good intentions for reading, and the books they would never get to this summer.

"You know I don't have time to read in the summer. I just come so I can talk to y'all and drink wine!" laughed Stacie. Murph and her husband had bought the beach house just beyond hers, by the boardwalk, and they had become beach friends when the couple was down from Elizabeth City on weekends. Sometimes their three precious tow-headed grandsons would be along, camped out under their large tent, building sandcastles and having a ball. Sue and her husband Paul were regular customers; their children were grown and gone and they had retired to the area a couple of years ago. Paul did consulting work for a commercial builder and Sue was a retired teacher. Just stopping by their table and visiting with them over the years, Stacie had struck up a solid friendship with them. "Did those lovely flowers come from your garden?" Stacie asked Sue, referring to the wild flower arrangement on the table beside a beautiful birthday cake that Nina was setting up with plates and forks for later.

"Yes," said Sue. "My garden's going *crazy* this summer with all the rain we've had. You need to come by and enjoy it. I'll cook for *you* for a change!"

Bets was the shortest and youngest member of their group, with a chic blonde haircut and engaging cornflower blue eyes. She had the most infectious laugh and a striking smile to match. Her skin was like porcelain since she hated to be outside, and God forbid, break a sweat! She and Stacie had met in the food business. Bets was a baker who worked from home, as a way to conduct her business and care for her four-year old daughter, Allie. Among other delights, she made beautiful cheesecakes she adorned with varieties of fresh fruits that were the talk of the island, and sold them to Stacie for her restaurant. "Let's go look at your cake," said Bets. "It's a masterpiece! I can't wait for you to see it…and taste it. It's lemon."

They wandered back into the dining room to admire the large, white cake, bordered in silver starfish with *Happy Birthday Stacie* written in silver script, a large starfish dotting the *i*, and other starfish scattered randomly about. "It's beautiful! Thank you, Bets!" Stacie breathed.

She went back out to join Tyson on the deck with her family and Kyle and Chelsea. Tyson took her arm and steered her toward the railing to lean with him and look out over the water. Several sailboats were moored beyond them, bobbing in the silvery moonlight. The moon was just rising, a huge silvery orb in the now deep blue sky. "You ended up with the perfect night for this party," she swooned to him, pressing her hand into the small of his back as he smiled at her.

"Well…lucky for you, it's a *blue moon*. It really couldn't be any more special than this…but how great is that on your big day?"

"What does that mean, a blue moon?"

"It's when there's a full moon twice in one month. It only happens rarely, and luckily, June 30th, your birthday, is the day this time."

Her eyebrows rose in wonder and he smiled at her again. "I think this will be an *exceptional* night for us," he said softly, stroking a stray strand of hair away from her eyes.

Andrew was sauntering toward them, carrying two martinis. Before he handed Stacie her pear martini, he said, "This is from Zack, but I'm going to need to see your ID first, miss!" When he grinned his boyish smile at her, she laughed as he handed Tyson his favorite dirty martini. They toasted, and several people standing near them wished her another "Happy birthday" as she sipped the heavenly drink, raising her glass to Zack, who stood with Nina at the bar.

She murmured into Tyson's ear, "Please don't let me get smashed tonight. I want to remember everything tomorrow."

He spoke into her hair, his lips touching her face, "Oh, I promise…I want you to remember all of it, too!"

The Mary Washington girls appeared before them with platters of appetizers for them to taste—crab-stuffed mushrooms, crispy small, phyllo shells with pecan chicken salad, and shrimp cocktail skewers.

"Oh, my!" murmured Stacie. "This is incredible. Who's in there cooking all this?"

"Sanders and Darius are back there, sticking it all in the oven. We put it together earlier today when your mom and dad took you guys to lunch," said Tyson, winking at her. Sanders, a student at Old Dominion University, was the breakfast cook and crew chief, who shared Tyson's passion for surfing on his afternoons off. Darius was part of the breakfast crew as well.

"Well, this is so nice. And girls you look great! You sure clean up good!" she laughed with them. It was unusual to see them, hair loose in the breeze and dressed in their lovely short dresses instead of the typical *The Sound Side* T-shirts and shorts they wore to work.

"Happy birthday! You look so good, yourself!" said Kate. "I hope I look that good in twenty years!" she gushed and the other girls grimaced, Alex's dark eyes opening wide at the faux-pas, as they glanced at each other uneasily.

Stacie blinked, "Ouch, Kate! Let's just say nineteen years. You're twenty-one, right? Twenty years just sounds *way* too real for me right now."

Kate's eyes cut to the floor, and then to the other girls. "Sorry, I was just using a round figure, I guess," she said, sheepishly.

"And no *round figure* jokes for the forty-year old either!" Stacie laughed, good-naturedly, and the girls laughed with her.

"Not like you're anywhere near *round*," Lilia smiled at her and Tyson winked at her again.

"I'm going to check on Sanders in the kitchen," Tyson said, draining his martini glass and offering to take hers.

She wandered over to the picnic table where Shelly sat with their mother and the Duck girls. The talk was about Kyle and his lovely girlfriend. Her mother Elaine was speaking to Shelly about Chelsea. "She's very special. I believe she's brought out the best in Kyle. They certainly seem star-crossed, don't you think?" They turned to look at Kyle and Chelsea, who were engaged in conversation with some of the other young waiters and kitchen staff on the deck, overlooking the water. At that moment, Kyle's eyes flickered over Chelsea, and he caught her hand. He glanced at her, pulling her away from the group, steering her toward the railing, speaking to her in her ear, and she closed her eyes for a moment and said something back to him, reaching for his face.

Shelly nodded and said to her mother, "Yes, she's had quite an effect on both of us. She helped us put our lives back together, just by being her."

"Well, I can see such a big difference in all of you. I'm glad I was able to come up here when you had your surgery so he could go up to the mountains and be with her after her grandmother died."

"I know. We all appreciate that, Mom. Miss Kitty was a really special lady."

"I remember meeting her and Mr. Davenport one Christmas when we were there. She was a lovely person, and such a funny lady! They had a brunch at their house, remember, Shelly? It was before he died and years before her stroke," said Elaine. "Chelsea was just a little girl then. I remember her, too."

"I miss Liz and Tom so much already," said Shelly, referring to Chelsea's parents, her dear friends from early in her marriage to Stuart Davis. Tom had been Stu's business partner when they first moved to the mountains, when all Stu's troubles began. "We'll have to get that guest room up to snuff so they can visit soon."

"We will," Elaine promised her, "but right now I want to hear about the birthday girl. What have you been doing?"

Stacie recalled her encounter with Rick at the bank the other day and told them triumphantly of her grand tell-off. They hooted in delight at the story.

"Oh, *Rick the Prick!*" Sue said, making them all laugh. Then Sue put her hand to her mouth apologetically. "I'm sorry, Elaine! It's just what we've always called him. Didn't Tyson come up with it?"

Stacie laughed. "No, actually, Tyson calls him *Rick the Dick*."

Bets threw her head back and cackled loudly.

Elaine joined her. "It's okay. It's a lovely sentiment!" she said, raising her glass of white wine, and they returned her toast.

"To Rick the Dick!" laughed Sue before they sipped their drinks. "Oh, my! The last time we had a great party like this was at your divorce party, here!" said Sue. Stacie stole a glance at Shelly, remembering the party, a year after Desiree's death, when Stacie realized that Stu was having major alcohol problems.

"Tyson can throw a great party!" said Murph. "It was a wonderful celebration! I have to say, though, Rick was good for one or two things, like fixing up this place into The Sound Side."

"Yeah, he might have financed it, but Stacie made it the special place it is," said Bets.

"Well, he was never really into it like I was," explained Stacie. "He just indulged me on this project. He took one look at this place and thought it was the biggest dump. He always wanted something slicker, more upscale. I'm glad he moved on to Pompano's and left me The Sound Side. It's *my* little slice of heaven."

"And the house…I like the house!" said Murph. "We never would have met if he hadn't given you the house."

"I know…I really got off good with that whole deal," said Stacie wistfully. They were all quiet a moment; the bitterest of all those memories was best left unspoken.

"Well, you wouldn't have Tyson either if the prick had stuck around," said Shelly, uncharacteristically, and they all laughed again. "He's so fantastic, Stacie. He's perfect for you."

"I know," she groaned, and they laughed again. "It was a blessing in disguise, how it all worked out."

"You deserve a second chance, you know?" Shelly told her, pointedly.

"So what kind of diet have you been on, sweetheart? You're almost *too* thin," her mother said, a look of concern crossing her eyes briefly.

Stacie rolled her eyes and steeled herself for the inevitable conversation. "It's these iron supplements my doctor has me taking. I feel like I want to vomit half the time. I can't eat when I'm taking them."

"Oh, *honey*, are you still having problems?" her mother asked, her brows furrowed in worry.

"I don't know. I have to go in next week for an exam. I'm thinking I have fibroids again."

"Is she thinking about doing a hysterectomy?"

Stacie shook her head. It wasn't news to any of the women sitting at the tables; they watched for her reaction.

"It's a possibility at this point. I'm almost ready just to get it over with, you know? I've had two surgeries already. I'm just sick of it. I'd like to just…feel good again."

"Well, your job is so stressful, especially in the summer," Elaine continued. "You work too hard."

"I know. If I did anything it would have to be after Thanksgiving…" Stacie mumbled, and the perky young college girls were there again, displaying crab dip and pita points with little plates, and another martini for Stacie courtesy of Zack. Then it was time for singing and the delicious birthday cake that Nina and Bets served for all the guests. Sanders had emerged from the kitchen in his turned around baseball cap and gauged earrings, announcing that the kitchen staff promised her she could sleep-in the next morning while they handled breakfast without her.

Kyle was in front of her and reached for her hand. "Hey, birthday girl! Can I steal you away for a minute?" he asked, grinning and flashing his blue eyes at her.

"Sure!" she said. They went to sit on one of the benches by the deck railing.

"I haven't had a chance to talk to you all night!" he said, giving her shoulders a hug.

"Oh, honey, you're the best person I know!" she said, squeezing his solid, square, tanned face in her hand.

His eyebrows shot up in surprise. "Wow, I'm outranking Tyson! That's impressive! How many martinis have you *had?*" he laughed.

"Well…" she reconsidered. "He's *always* at the top of my list, but you're right up there. It's just that you've really pulled yourself together, and I'm so proud of you," she said, suddenly filled with emotion from being with him, after thinking about his situation and his previous visit with Chelsea and Shelly at spring break, when all the mysteries and secrets had surfaced and he and his mother had resolved their differences. "You've become such a good man. I love you so much."

"The feeling's mutual," he said, holding her hand and smiling at her. "Look, I'm sorry I won't be here helping you out that much this summer. I'll be leaving tomorrow for freshman orientation with Mom and Pops, and then I have to be back at UVA on the first of August for football practice. That hardly leaves me a month. I might need to head up to the mountains one last time before Chelsea and I go to school, too, you know, for her birthday?"

"Hey, it's fine. We'll manage! I just worry about that blessed girl you'll be leaving behind!"

When he looked down, she regretted saying it that way. "I'm sorry, I just meant…she's so great, and I know you're both so much in love. Seriously, you should just take her and…take her!" she said, gesturing into the air.

He looked up at her incredulously.

She blinked at him. "You *have*, right?"

He reddened. "Just once. The night she got here, before Gran came. I mean, it wasn't like Mom could come chasing after us with her cast, you know? She was pretty much down for the count with one of her Vicadin."

"Right under Shelly's very roof?" Stacie gasped. "You've got *way* more nerve than I gave you credit for!" she laughed, watching Chelsea, who was deep in conversation with Lilia and Alex by the kitchen. Her eyes flickered to Kyle for a moment and she returned her attention to Lilia's story. "Are you using protection?" Stacie asked him urgently.

"Yeah…she's been on the pill for over a year. It's something about female stuff and her complexion."

"I can relate to that," Stacie sighed, "but are y'all being safe?"

He looked at her indulgently. "Damn, do I have to spell it out for you? We were both virgins…" he said, his voice drifting off.

Her face lit into a huge smile. "I guess I should have known that. Do you have your key to my house, still?"

"Sure," he said. "Do you need me to go get something for you?"

"No…look, I hate to see a girl hyperventilate like that. She almost passes out every time you touch her. You should go to my house after Mom and Dad take Shelly home. You can have *one hour* and then you both turn into pumpkins. Your old room, *not* mine! And make the bed."

He shook his head at her, "Are you serious? My mom would *shit* if she heard this."

"I know, so shut up and don't tell her. I've had way too many martinis, right?"

"Yeah, that must be it," he laughed as Chelsea joined them and sat beside Stacie on the other side of the bench. Her black, lace-backed tank top over her white Capri pants made her look sophisticated and unusually beautiful. Her hair was swept to one side in a low pony tail, making more visible a little silver star necklace that sparkled at her collarbone as it caught the moonlight.

"Happy birthday!" she said, hugging Stacie. "You look like you're having such a great time! You have a glow about you tonight!" Chelsea said excitedly, glancing at Kyle and smiling.

"Really?" asked Stacie and they both nodded. Tyson wandered up to them as some of the guests were beginning to collect themselves, preparing to leave.

"Shelly's getting ready to go," he said to her. "She says she's kind of hit the wall, you know?"

"Sure. I'm surprised she's made it this long," Stacie said, raising her eyebrows to Kyle and standing to say goodbye to her family.

Later that night, on the porch outside her living room, Stacie found Tyson, leaning out over the railing, stretched comfortably with his arms hanging over the edge, the blue moon bathing him in silvery light. She ran her hands up his back, from his waist to his shoulders, massaging the base of his neck.

"Don't stop!" he moaned and stretched into her reach, taking all he could.

"Thank you so much for my party…you really outdid yourself. I had such a great time and all the right people were there. It was fabulous… and the food….There's nothing sexier to me than a man who can cook!"

"Mmmm, keep talking," he said, wrapping her into his warm body and breathing in the scent of her. "You just…leave me breathless," he whispered into her ear and kissed her, sliding his hands up and down her body, from her hips to her neck, taking her mouth into his and kissing her again. "There's only one more thing that would make this night perfect," he murmured into her hair.

"I think that's *next*," she whispered back to him, sliding her hands inside his shirt and letting her fingers caress the muscles across his back.

"Actually, I had something else in mind," he said, turning slightly away from her, his green eyes sparkling at her in the moonlight, which piqued her attention. "I haven't given you your present yet."

"Not another apron, please!" she begged.

He laughed, reaching into his pocket and producing a small, aqua box, tied with a white ribbon, and set it on the railing, glancing at her for her reaction.

As her hand went to her mouth, she gasped softly, looking at him incredulously. "*Tiffany's?*"

"I told you I was good with money," he said, modestly. "All I need is a roof over my head, a surfboard, and you, baby. Will you *please* marry me, damn it?" he asked with tortured green eyes.

Her slow smile spread across her face and she took his jaw in her palm, pulling his face to hers, kissing him desperately. "Yes!" she murmured into his mouth, and she felt him melt into her, wrapping his arms around her again, kissing her over and over.

She pulled away from him and smiled, tugging at the white ribbon on the box, slipping the aqua paper off of it and opening the box, revealing a sparkling, small, cushion cut diamond ring, set in a band of tiny diamonds, catching the blue moonlight like nothing she had ever seen before. She stared, open mouthed, and looked up at him. He took the box from her and took the ring, sliding it onto her finger, holding her hand up to the moon and kissing her hand, with his eyes closed.

"It's perfect," she breathed, her head swimming as he steadied her, pulling her into him again and kissing her.

He looked at the ring on her finger and twisted it back and forth, frowning. "It's a little big, don't you think?" he said, curiously. "Aren't you a five and a half?"

"Hmmm, I was. I didn't realize I'd lost this much weight."

"It's not a problem. We can get it sized."

"I don't know…I don't think I'm ever taking this off!" she laughed and then looked at him seriously. "I love you so much. I would *love* to marry you…and be your wife, and be yours forever."

"Let's go make a baby," he said, kissing her forehead and holding her close. *The clock is ticking*, she thought, dreamily, allowing herself to be swept up in his arms and carried into the bedroom.

Chapter 3

DECISIONS

The following Wednesday during their break between lunch and dinner, Tyson and Stacie lay relaxing on the beach near the dunes by her house. She held her hand out in front of her, letting the sunlight catch the diamonds in her ring, sending little rainbows scattering across the sand dune in front of them. They had called their families with the news on Monday morning, before Chelsea left, and Kyle, Shelly, and her father took off for UVA while Elaine went back to Charlotte. No plans had been made, but their news had been well-received. Now, he lazed beside her, propped on one elbow, tracing his finger slowly down the shallow cleft between her abdominal muscles and letting it linger at her navel, splaying his fingers across the roundness of her belly, playing at the edge of her bathing suit.

"So you were too tired to surf today?" she asked, shielding her eyes with her hand.

"Yeah…maybe if I would *sleep* at night instead of staying up all night having the best sex of my life…I wouldn't be so tired," he said, contentedly, a smile in his voice.

"Well, we might as well rest today. We should have a really busy weekend, too," she said, referring to the upcoming holiday, starting tomorrow with the Fourth of July.

"Are you planning on hiring another bartender?" he asked.

"Yeah, I've had some people come by already to apply. Word gets around, doesn't it? I'll help Zack and Andrew out tomorrow night and the rest of the weekend, until I can get somebody with some experience in place. I'm done training people at this point in the summer."

She had been forced to fire Kate, who, as it turned out, was not twenty-one after all. "So what was it that tipped you off about her being under-age?" he asked curiously.

"It was that comment she made at my party about me being twenty years older…and the way the other girls reacted. And then I checked her file on a hunch, and sure enough, her birth date on her job application showed that she's only twenty."

"But didn't you check her ID when she said she wanted to bartend?"

"I did, but it's a fake."

"Hmmm, that's a major character flaw. It's one thing to be giving away drinks for free, but another thing for her to lie about her age. That's going to catch up with her eventually," he commented.

"I know. It's a shame, too. I really like Kate…and usually, I think I'm a pretty good judge of character. Normally, the problems I have are people showing up late or taking out the wrong food, or forgetting someone's order—never dishonesty."

They were quiet for a moment, enjoying the balmy breeze that blew over them, cooling their hot skin and lulling them into peacefulness. As she listened to the gentle waves, she asked, "So, tell me again why you love surfing so much?"

He thought about it for a moment and took her hand before answering her. "It's a lot like making love. It's like being on top of a woman, rising and falling with her…and even when she drags you down, hard across the floor of the sea, you just get back up and do it again, waiting for that big wave that makes it all worth it. It's the same way I feel about you, you know. You could just throw me around as much as you wanted and I'd be back for more. It's… just hopeless."

"Hmm," she said. "And will you still feel this way when I'm old and wrinkled and pudgy?"

He touched his fingertip to the lines at the outer corner of her left eye. "Do you mean, when I'm going bald and I have a beer belly and saggy eyelids?" She made a horrified face. "I told you, I'm willing to let you drag me around on the ocean floor. I don't guess it matters what we look like. I love you for all of time. Maybe you should give *me* a ring if it would help you to understand that."

"Mmm. I will be doing that soon…Where have you been all of my life?" she said in wonder. "There were never guys like you when I was younger. I always went for the bad boys."

"Lucky for me. And I'm lucky I ended up here to find you. How unlikely is that, you know?"

"Why didn't you settle down before this?"she asked curiously.

"We've been through this before, and it's still amazingly simple. I just didn't like the women I was meeting, or the places I was staying. I know what I want. If it wasn't right, it wasn't right. I just knew it and kept moving."

"Not everyone is that brave…" she said, her voice trailing off.

"I think *you* were brave…to go off on your own and take over The Sound Side like you did. And then you added breakfast…you're either really brave or really crazy!"

She laughed out loud. "Not so brave as just getting dumped on my ass! And I had to add breakfast to make money…and to have a place to hide out."

"Who're you hiding from, Rick the Dick?"

She smiled, "Yeah, I guess. I just can't even stand looking at him…or smelling him," she said, crossing her arm over her eyes to shield them from the sun, while hearing him laugh softly beside her.

"I just know when I walked into the marina that day and saw you standing in the kitchen sweeping, in your white apron, and you looked at me with those big blue eyes, I was sunk…Rick or no Rick. I'm glad I was smart enough to hang around and bide my time. God, I *knew* you didn't belong with him."

That had been three years ago, when things had quickly unraveled. Rick had gotten tired of The Sound Side and her vision of what it could be. He went on to find another restaurant to open and eventually another lover to stroke his ego. She had counted on Tyson to command the kitchen while she took control of the business end of the operation, managing the bar and the dining room, the finances and the music, auditioning and scheduling bands. She had not had much of a life outside the restaurant, and she had joked to him that it kept her out of trouble, being so absorbed. Her staff was loyal and top notch, becoming her family. Everyone who worked for her had been consumed in her passion for the place until it quickly became a diamond in the rough on the back end of the island. It attracted just the right laid-back crowd she wanted, the food was excellent, and the music buffs were regulars every Friday and Saturday night. The kitchen would close around ten o'clock when the bands would take the little stage and the magic would begin.

As her divorce dragged on, Stacie had known Tyson was interested in her, but she couldn't bring herself to get involved again so soon, and he played it cool for the sake of their working relationship which was excellent. When Kyle had come to stay with her the previous summer, she had found a side of herself she didn't know existed. She had felt such a yearning to nurture him, yet realized he needed a firm hand to keep him on track. Tyson watched them, admiring the way she was able to balance one more thing in her already busy life, and do it so well. He developed his own friendship with Kyle, discovering a kindred spirit in the troubled teen. He offered to take Kyle surfing as a way to calm him down from the anger and sooth the depression he was experiencing. It seemed to help him unwind and relax. Stacie was riveted to their connection, and the three of them had quickly formed a bond, an odd camaraderie for three people aged thirty-nine, thirty, and seventeen. Kyle never spoke about his problems, but he seemed to find a peaceful place to float for a while. And within that year, after Kyle left, she let herself open up to Tyson Garrett and fell deeply and unconditionally in love with him.

They were quiet for awhile, listening to the soft, slow swooshing of the waves, and she thought about the discussion they had had, trying to make their plans. Neither of them wanted a big wedding, perhaps just the families, but then, their friends would kill them. Everyone was so happy for them, and all of them were taking credit for moving them along in the right direction. A small family wedding at the little chapel by the sea would be just the thing, and then they could have a huge party at The Sound Side afterwards. Kyle had wanted the South Street band to play for the party, and he had made sure Stacie knew it before he left for freshman orientation. She smiled and sighed. Weddings were often about pleasing everyone else. She had skipped all that once, marrying Rick in Las Vegas, which as everyone reminded her, had been the first mistake she'd made with him. The second was staying with him for seven years. Maybe now it would be a good thing to please the people who meant so much to her and were planning on supporting both of them in this journey.

"What are you thinking about?" he asked, from under the shade of his hand.

"Just how much fun this wedding will be, no matter how large or small it turns out. It's just nice to have everyone's support. Will your family come down from Cape May?"

"Yeah, definitely. I'm sure my parents will be here…and my brothers.

My brothers need to meet you soon. Henry's in school at NYU right now, and Jesse works in the maritime museum at home. He and his wife, Mel, will come for sure. You'll like her. She's pretty chill. I'd like them to meet you before the wedding. They're all really excited. I guess they thought this wasn't happening for me, being the oldest and all," he said wryly. "Although, my mother says she wasn't a bit surprised."

"I *love* your mother," Stacie said emphatically. "She's a ball of fire, and she is so proud of you."

"Well, last year when they came down here to visit, you couldn't have been a bigger hit. They loved you too…who wouldn't? But you impressed them with your success at the business. And they're glad I've found the right niche for myself as a chef. They're just glad that I'm happy."

She had wondered whether they minded that he was her employee and that she was older, but they didn't seem to be fazed, as he had never been. She didn't think of him as any of that either, but it was hard to know how secure other people were in themselves. Now if she could get him to be comfortable living in *her* house.…

That evening at dinner, Stacie visited with the crowd at her favorite table, the Murphys, Bets and Jim, the island vet, and Sue and Paul. They had all come in to see her and celebrate her engagement to Tyson, who had even made a special appearance himself, bringing them an appetizer earlier and chatting at the table. As she walked over to the bar to check on Andrew and Zack, Nina gave her a worried look and raised her eyebrows toward the bar. She looked over and saw a familiar figure sitting at the bar, talking to Zack and laughing, then taking a pull off of an Amstel Light. Rick had not been in the place in over two years, and her breath caught as a strange déjà-vu took her by surprise. He wore his purple striped shirt open at the collar with the sleeves rolled up and dark jeans with dark brown leather boat shoes. His dark hair had been cut since she had seen him that day at the bank and it was gelled in place. He wore a military style black watch on his wrist and his large platinum wedding band glistened in the low lights at the bar. She remembered to close her mouth before he turned around, lest he think she was gawking at him and get the wrong idea. Zack had caught her eye and winked slightly while Andrew looked on protectively, as if waiting to pick her up if she were to fall on her face. She straightened her soft gray sundress as she made her way toward the bar.

"Hello, Rick. What a surprise!" she said, pleasantly, as if he were any other customer out for a beer on a Wednesday evening. She sniffed and wrinkled her nose impulsively at the strong cologne. Andrew noticed and smirked imperceptibly to anyone else but her. "Are you off tonight?" she asked Rick as he took her in, looking her up and down with his large brown eyes, smiling at her. His eyes, after taking in the silver hoops at her ears and the deep V neck of the dress, grew larger as he looked into her face openly.

"Hello. How are you, Stacie? You're looking good. Actually, I'm here on business."

She glanced back at the table she had just left and got a vague impression of all six of her friends craning their necks for the best view.

"The place looks great!" he said sincerely. She saw Zack beam proudly, but Andrew was undecided, pressing his lips together and watching her guardedly. "You did it the way you wanted, and it's turned out really well," he remarked, casting his eyes around and pumping his head.

She refused to let him see her irritation. She laughed her throaty laugh, letting her eyes twinkle at him, just a little, playing with his head. "So what's up? What brings you to The Sound Side?" she asked, leaning against the bar and resting her elbow on the old, smooth mahogany.

"I had a girl stop by today looking for a job," he said, running a hand over his fashionable day old stubble. "She didn't give your name as a reference, but one of the kids said she had worked over here this summer." *One of the kids*, she thought. At one time Torie was *one of the kids* before he'd started screwing her in the office. "Her name is Kate something," he said, small lines appearing at the outer corners of his eyes.

Stacie raised her eyebrows. "She did work here until Monday night. What kind of job is she applying for?"

"She wants to wait tables. Did she get fired?"

"Yes, she did."

"Should I hire her? You don't trust her. I can tell."

"Do what you want. She was one of my bartenders, but she lied about her age. She's not twenty-one. She has a fake ID, but she put down her real birthday on her application. Maybe she's learned her lesson. I thought she was a good worker. People like her and she shows up."

He nodded, seeming satisfied. "Okay. Good to know."

Her friends were leaving and stopped by to get a hug from her on their way out the door, congratulating her and telling her to give Tyson their best, quite enthusiastically. And then Rick saw the ring sparkling on her finger.

He cocked his head back and the little lines around his eyes appeared again. "Ah, I see you have news," he said, taking her hand and examining the ring. "Nice," he said, turning her hand in the light. He continued to torture her with his presence. He could easily have called or sent one of his "kids" to come snooping.

She reddened suddenly, wondering whether he would make some gauche remark about her having paid for it in the long run, being the boss. But he did not, and looked up at her, confusing her, scorching her face further, under her bartenders' scrutiny. "So you're happy?" he asked quietly; she nodded, angry, wishing he would leave. "Good. You deserve it," he said and drained the rest of his beer, setting it back on the bar ledge and sliding off the stool. "Thanks for the tip. Take care, Stacie. Congratulations. Thanks, Zack!" he called and waved to Zack who had discreetly removed himself to the opposite end of the bar. And Rick was out the door.

On Friday, Stacie visited her doctor on her break. Karen Walters was attractive in a no-nonsense professional way, and tall and personable, with a caring bedside manner, probing turquoise eyes, and a quick and engaging laugh. They had joked that if they were both available on the day after July Fourth, then neither of them had much of a life! Karen had been Stacie's doctor since she had had the miscarriage in the second year of her marriage, when they had discovered that uterine fibroid tumors had caused it. It had been a devastating experience altogether, learning of her pregnancy and realizing how upset Rick had been about it. He had been so relieved when she miscarried, telling her he had never wanted children in the first place and that maybe it was a sign that it just wasn't in the cards for them.

She did not tell Tyson about her appointment and went over to the office as soon as lunch was over. Karen was thrilled with her engagement news and the whole conversation they had following her check-up was different than what Stacie had prepared herself for. After two surgeries to remove the fibroids over the years, Stacie was expecting Karen to recommend a hysterectomy, but as Karen held her hand and gazed at the lovely ring, she took a deep breath and said, "Okay, I guess we need to discuss your options."

Karen told her that pregnancy was not out of the question, but presented significant risks, as the uterine wall became compromised with scarring from each of the surgeries. Stacie would need additional surgery before trying to conceive, unless it happened immediately, and they would watch her carefully if she became pregnant. She might have to reduce her workload and delegate some of the restaurant responsibilities to other employees. Or she could go ahead with the hysterectomy and be done with it.

"What would you do if it were you?" Stacie asked.

Karen popped a large sigh from between her lips. "Well, since I'm older than you and married with the best daughter on earth, and if I'd been through all the pain you've been through, I'd *yank it*, personally. But you have a chance, not a great chance, but a chance at having a baby—one baby, and that would be your little miracle. Having one child is so worth it, Stacie. But it might not be for you with the kind of life you lead. Believe me; I know how hard it was for us. You have a big decision to make. I think you should talk it over with Tyson. Go ahead and have your surgery…and then I wouldn't wait long if you decide to get pregnant. Call your mother. Let me know what you decide."

The sky was clouding up and a warm breeze blew over her as she drove back to the restaurant in the Cabrio, mulling it all over. She checked her watch. Four o'clock. Tyson would be there first, so she could talk to him before anyone else came in. She couldn't wait to tell him the news. She could imagine the look on his face. She could imagine him taking her in his arms and holding her on his lap. He would be so happy. He would tell her he loved her. She had never had a chance like this before. After the summer season was over, she would eliminate breakfast altogether from the business and cut back on her hours. Zack was perfectly capable of running the bar, and Nina the dining room. Tyson definitely had the kitchen under control without her, and she could do the music business by Skype on her computer with her feet propped up at home. She had never felt this good, so happy before. Her life was finally becoming what she'd dreamed about.

As she pulled into the parking lot, she saw Tyson's truck and noticed his new air-brushed painting on the back of his tailgate. Andrew had created a beautiful scene with silhouetted ducks rising from a marsh in a golden sky on the dark cherry red of the truck. He did air-brushed art as his day job at one of the local surf shops, and he had moonlighted for her the last couple of years. A red BMW was parked two spaces down that she recognized as Kate's car. Friday was pay-day and she was probably stopping by to pick up her last check as the others would be soon. It was a sad state of affairs when the help drove nicer vehicles than the owners. Oh well, she loved her car, ten years old as it was. She zipped into her regular parking space and trotted up the steps, swinging her yellow purse over her shoulder, hearing reggae music playing from the kitchen. Tyson must be in a good mood after a little surfing this afternoon at the pier.

The music was turned up loud the way he liked it when nobody was around to complain. She went into the office to drop her bag and see whether he was in there. And he was, standing against the wall with Kate barely an inch away from him, her mouth open on his, his hands pushing her arms away from him, her hand at his waist, trying to pull him closer to her. He opened his eyes, saw Stacie, and pushed Kate off of him, swearing and running his hand across the back of his neck. Kate whirled around and gasped, her eyebrows shooting up into dark double arches, wiping her mouth with the back of her hand.

Stacie stood motionless as Kate collected herself, smoothing her loose blonde hair and straightening her hot pink tank top over the top of her short skirt. "Oh, my God! I'm…so sorry!" she murmured, casting her eyes nervously about, stepping away from Tyson, and grabbing her colorful designer handbag off the desk. Finally, she looked at Stacie.

"Did you get what you came for?" Stacie asked roughly, lifting her chin confrontationally.

Kate picked up the envelope off the desk and moved toward the door that Stacie occupied. "I'm so sorry! This was my fault. He didn't do anything."

"Get out," Stacie ordered.

"But, don't…."

"Get the hell out of my restaurant," Stacie said. Kate slipped by her and was gone. In a moment, they could hear the BMW growl to life and tires spin out of the shelled parking lot. Stacie felt herself transcend her body as if she were floating several feet in the air. Her face flamed. Tyson stared at her, deep set green eyes searching hers. It had been minutes and neither of them had spoken.

"What the hell was that?" Stacie murmured hoarsely.

"She…came in here to get her paycheck. I gave it to her," he said as if recounting a crime for a detective. "I gave her a hug, and then she was kissing me…" he said looking at her for help. "I was trying to tell her to stop."

"Really? In what language? Usually when you have your tongue down *my* throat, it means something entirely different!"

"*She* put her tongue in *my* mouth, thanks," he said indignantly. "Oh, come on, Stace! She was here all of…five minutes?"

"And that's all it took? Wow, it's a good thing I got here when I did! Just think what could have happened!" she said, sinking down into the chair in front of her desk, her purse sliding to the floor. Suddenly she felt so old and so tired. "I can't believe this is happening again…" she whispered, putting her hand to her head. The reggae music seemed too loud and inappropriate.

"What?" he said, leaning forward, placing the palms of his hands flat on her desk and trying to make eye contact with her. "We just had this discussion the other day. Whose character is on the line here, hers or mine?"

She looked at him, speechless. All she could see was Rick and Torie in virtually the same spot, with a few less articles of clothing, and not being able to separate themselves quite as quickly.

He shifted his weight from one foot to the other. He had been there that day too, so he had some idea of what she was imagining. "Okay. Listen," he said to her softly. "I made a mistake. A *small* mistake, but I should never have let this happen. I'm *sorry*. But I'm not Rick. Don't *do this*!"

She stared at the floor, wanting to believe him, wishing she could get the happiness back she had felt ten minutes ago, but she was floundering. He walked around to the front of the desk and sat on it, looking at her helplessly. They heard people bumping in through the front door, Zack and Nina, talking and laughing.

"You know I love you. I didn't want to hurt you…can we just go back ten minutes? This is insane!" he whispered. "Come on; we're getting married. We're going to have a baby…."

She looked at him remorsefully. "Then you never should have kissed one."

He breathed in sharply and set his jaw. She saw the hurt pass across his eyes. She had never seen that on his face before; it stung her. He pressed his lips together and nodded. He sighed and walked quietly out of the office. She buried her face in her hands and made her decision.

Yank it.

Chapter 4

Stormy Weather

It was a long Friday night. For the first time in almost three years, Stacie had wished she could have been anywhere but the restaurant. Thankfully, it was another busy holiday night and many of her friends were there for the music, and the place was loaded with tourists as well. Working in the bar with Zack and Andrew seemed to make the time go by faster, but still after the afternoon's events, it seemed agonizing. It was well after one-thirty when she had finalized her totals for the evening. She sat in the office by lamp light, paper-clipping some receipts together when Zack peeked in around the door. "You almost done?" he asked.

"Yeah," she said, distractedly, her hand in her hair, not realizing the time. "Are we the last ones?"

"I think so. Andrew and Tyson are in the parking lot looking at his truck. Do you have the deposit for me to drop off?"

"Sure. If you don't feel like going, I can do it tomorrow. I'll just stick it in the safe."

"No, it's fine. I'll go tonight," Zack said shrugging.

"You packing?"

"Always. Seriously, it's not a problem. I'm not tired."

"Okay, well, thanks," she said looking away from his probing eyes. Some of them had sensed that things weren't quite right, but she was not prepared to deal with it yet. She reached into the desk drawer and pulled out the money pouch she had just finished counting and handed it to him. Zack was the best. She depended on him to be not only her bar manager, but her bouncer, bodyguard, and bank courier as well. He had a concealed weapons permit, and she felt safer sending him to the bank when they closed. Still, she worried about him. And Nina was usually with him since they lived together. "Hang on a sec and I'll walk out with you."

He waited, watching her collect her purse and switch off the lamp. She checked around the other areas for locked doors and lights. Everything was taken care of, thanks probably to Zack and Tyson. Zack held the kitchen door for her as she locked the office deadbolt, then locked the front door. They walked out to the parking lot where Nina was standing with Andrew and Tyson at the back of Tyson's Chevy truck, admiring Andrew's latest artwork. Nina joined Zack, taking his hand and bidding the rest of them goodnight as they climbed into his car and zipped out of the lot into the night.

Stacie noticed that the frogs and crickets were exceptionally loud tonight as she stepped over to where the men were standing behind the truck. Andrew had been wiping the dew off the tailgate with a soft rag, and a cigarette dangled from the corner of his mouth. Tyson said nothing as the moment became awkward. He knew she wasn't having his sulking behavior. "This is beautiful, Andrew. I saw it this afternoon when I pulled in."

He smiled, taking a pull off his cigarette. "Thanks. You should let me do something on the back of the Cabrio…something small. How about a blue moon over the dark water with a sailboat in the background? Or something…" he suggested.

Anything but a blue moon. Her once in a blue moon dream had evaporated into thin air, but she figured he thought he was onto something.

"Yeah, maybe…that sounds nice." Tyson glanced at her out of the corner of his eye. On any other given night, Andrew would have drifted away and let them slide off to their cars to kiss and get into their separate vehicles, driving away to her house in Duck. But tonight, Andrew slid his eyes back and forth at them as they made no move to connect or make eye contact; he looked confused, fishing his own keys out of his pocket. "Okay, well, goodnight," Stacie said to them both. Tyson looked at her directly, hands shoved deep into his pockets, and replied, unsmiling, "Night, Stace." She turned and walked to her car as he watched her get in safely and start her engine. Then as she drove away, he stepped to the door of his truck and climbed in.

Saturday was the busiest day they'd had all summer. She showed up in a black tank top and jeans and did not leave all day. The talk up and down the beach was about the storm, now called Abigail, coming in on Monday, and most of the tourists were having their last hurrah before packing up and evacuating the island on Sunday. Stacie had left her ring at home in its Tiffany's box on the bedside table, having rehearsed what she would say to Tyson if and when he noticed its absence. He was quieter than usual, which no one but Stacie would have noticed, most likely, and he did not smile at her, which they might have noticed. Kyle was back from freshman orientation at UVA, and both of them took turns distracting themselves, catching up with him, stealing little glances at each other.

Jerry, the fish guy, appeared at ten o'clock as he did every other day; the staff had a grand time announcing him, as if the court jester had arrived. "Jerry, the fish guy's here!" was passed throughout the restaurant like a gossip game. Stacie emerged from the dining room, wiping her hands on her white apron to greet him.

"Hey! What's kickin', chicken?" asked Jerry, a short, heavyset blonde man with a soul patch on his chin, grinning up at her, and setting his sunglasses on top of his head.

"Hey, Jer! What d'ya got for us today?" she asked as Tyson installed himself beside her as usual, which was the closest they had been to each other since Friday afternoon.

"I got red snapper, grouper, and flounder today, brought in last night."

As she and Tyson inspected the fish Jerry had brought in for them to examine, she noticed Tyson's eyes pass over her hands and linger on her empty ring finger. His eyes flickered momentarily to her face and then away. If so many people had not been around, she could have explained, but the moment wasn't right and she felt ashamed, seeing the ghost of the hurt expression pass over his face again. They decided on the grouper and flounder. They could always freeze the fish and use it after the storm had passed. She figured they would close on Monday, if the forecasters were right, and hopefully, would only lose one day's business.

When Bets Brantley arrived with her cheesecakes, it was a different story. After laying her parcels on the kitchen counter and greeting everyone, she launched into her explanation of why she had brought three cakes instead of four. "I figured you had used up all the others over the holiday weekend, and with this storm coming, I thought just three would hold you until next Saturday," she said. Then she gasped loudly, grabbing Stacie's left hand. "Oh, my God! Where's your ring?" she cried and looked from Stacie to Tyson and back to Stacie. Tyson appeared to be immersed in the she crab soup he was mixing, adding sherry and tasting it, carefully.

"I…I'm having it sized," Stacie lied. "I don't want it slipping off and going down a drain, or into somebody's martini tonight."

"Oh, good thinking," Bets said, looking quizzically at Stacie and sneaking a glance at Tyson.

"So are you sticking around for the storm, or are y'all heading inland?" Stacie deflected, placing a hand on her hip and looking concerned at her friend.

"We're going to my mother's. They're saying it's just going to be a Category 2, but it's a nice excuse to go and see her. Jim won't have any business so he might as well close the office. We'll be back as soon as it passes. I'll be calling you to check it out."

"Well, yes, do call me, or I'll call you when it's all over. I'll be here, battening down."

That evening, the bar was hopping and Stacie was pleased with the band and the crowd that showed up. Time flew by as she got into her rhythm with Zack and Andrew behind the bar. "Do you really think we need a third bartender?" she asked them as the kitchen closed for the evening.

"Hell, yeah, if it's a woman," Zack said. "Don't bother with another guy."

"Just some part-time girl," said Andrew. "I don't guess you noticed your fan club here tonight," he said, smiling at her. "You definitely need a woman to draw the men."

"I felt like I just got in the way most of the time," she said.

"No way. After we count the tips tonight, you'll see. You might even consider giving up your day job!" Zack winked at her.

Kyle and Tyson had taken seats at the end of the bar, and Zack moved toward the other end. "Here's two of your fans right now."

"What'll it be, gentlemen?" she said to them in her throaty voice with her most infectious smile. It worked on Kyle, but Tyson remained subdued, ordering a beer for himself while Kyle ordered a Coke. Sometimes at home they let Kyle drink a beer, but not here when the other underage staff was around. "What's up, guys?" she asked, suddenly feeling a desperate need to have Tyson look at her with his deep green eyes and produce the dimples she loved when he smiled at her.

"Surf's up," said Kyle, grinning at her, but as his eyes flicked toward Tyson, he noticed a change in Tyson's demeanor since they had entered the bar. More seriously, he said, "I guess Ty told you; we're heading to Buxton in the morning for some serious surfing."

She nodded, pretending she knew. "Good for y'all. Be careful. How's Shelly doing?"

"Good," said Kyle. "She wants y'all to come over for tacos tomorrow night."

Tyson started to tip his beer back in response to Stacie's questioning look. "You guys go on. I'm gonna hang at my place and start boarding up the windows. I'll come up Monday morning and help you out here," he said absently. Immediately, Kyle assessed the difference in his tone.

Stacie fought to save the situation. "Okay, thanks; that would be great. And you can count on me for tacos. Are you cooking?" she asked Kyle, smiling at him.

"Yup," he said. "And I want you to take a look at Chelsea's brother's band on Skype. They're playing at her house tomorrow night, and you could audition them if you have any spots left this summer."

She thought a moment. "Actually, I do have the last weekend in July open. Andrew said he would play and fill in if I don't have anybody. Maybe I'll have a new barmaid by then."

Tyson's eyes stared straight ahead as he took another pull off his beer bottle. He would never show interest in another of her barmaids again, she thought.

"What kind of music do they play?"

Kyle shrugged, "A little bluegrass, lots of popular stuff, and some of them do a Celtic set. They can do Christmas too, if you want Christmas in July…."

Stacie wrinkled her nose, "Don't think so. Can they play for two hours?"

"Yeah. I've heard them several times. I think you'll really like them. They're called Bangelic…it's the Celtic thing," he said, shrugging.

"Cool," she said, nodding, while noticing Tyson drain his beer bottle.

"So…everything's set back in the kitchen, boss. You need anything?" he asked coolly.

She hesitated, wanting to tell him what she needed, but his eyes were telling her he was done.

"No. I'm good…if you need to go. I'll see you on Monday morning, then."

"Okay…goodnight then," he said pleasantly, and clasped Kyle's hand in a high five. "See you at eight at Sam and Omie's, dude." He slapped Kyle on the back and was off the barstool and out the front door, waving at some of the guys on his way out, pulling car keys out of his pocket, and running a hand through his black curls. He looked exhausted, as if he had not slept. She thought about him going home to his messy little duplex with the good kitchen, scattered and strewn with books, and crashing on the bed with his clothes on.

Kyle's hand was propping up his chin on the bar, and his blue eyes were burning a hole through Stacie. "What?" she asked in exasperation.

"What's going on with you two?"

"Nothing is going on."

"Like hell. He looks like somebody just ran over his dog. And since he doesn't have a dog, I figure it's got something to do with you."

"Well, aren't you just jumping to conclusions? You weren't this smart till you met Chelsea," she muttered, walking down the bar and waiting on some other customers.

"So what has he told you?" she asked when she came back.

"Nothing. The guy's a tomb. You know he'd never say a bad thing about you," Kyle replied, waiting for her response. She rolled her eyes and her face flamed.

"That's because *he* did something, not *me*."

Kyle's eyebrows went up a notch. "How bad could it be?"

"I saw him kissing Kate…or Kate kissing him, and I walked in on it."

Enlightenment broke over his face. "Oh, right. That was why she got fired…."

"No, actually, she lied about being twenty-one; that was why she got fired. The kissing thing was after."

Stacie was called away by several men who had come up and wanted to talk to her. When she returned, Kyle's Coke was finished so she refreshed it. "That's it for you," she warned him, kiddingly.

"So…what, you're not getting married anymore? Just because of that? Even *I* know it didn't mean anything," he said, looking at her suspiciously. "Aren't you gonna give him a do-over at least? I mean, come on, it's *Tyson*! He's like…perfect with you. Didn't you learn anything from me this year? You know, forgiveness and all?"

She dissolved, seeing his kindred blue eyes bore into hers with an intensity she didn't know young people possessed. She started to understand what he and Chelsea had between them.

"Forgiveness is easy. Trust is harder. But I know…I'm being an idiot. I just…it just took me back to a place I thought I'd left. It took me back to when I found Rick cheating on me. It was even in the same place—my office. It hurt a lot. There's more going on with me than you need to know right now."

He nodded, "Okay, fair enough. But don't hurt him. He's my friend. And he loves you. Don't be stupid."

On Sunday, Stacie slept until eleven o'clock after a night of tossing and turning. Then she had coffee on the porch in her bathrobe, looking out across the dunes at the sea, which seemed much closer than usual, with its high swells and loud crashing waves. The sea was acting much like her heart at the moment, churning restlessly and violently. She knew it was pointless to try and walk on the beach since the sand would assault her like needles in this wind. The Murphys had not made it down for the weekend due to the impending storm, so she missed seeing Lucy and catching up with her over the week, although she was glad to avoid questions about the ring's absence on her finger, and the look in her eyes that her dear friend would be sure to scrutinize.

She spent the afternoon going for groceries, things she would not need to heat up in case she lost power, and she bought nails at the hardware store for boarding up her windows. The wood was stowed in her shed below the house, and she wondered whom she could get to help her batten down the hatches, now that Tyson was not presently in her picture. She would ask Kyle at dinner. His father had had him swinging a hammer from the time he was twelve. A deep sadness crept into her heart, knowing all this heartache could have been avoided, had Tyson not made his small mistake, and had she not reacted the way she had. And what had caused that? It was more than just the déjà-vu experience of reliving Rick's blatant affair in front of her and her employees that day, awful as it was. It was their whole failed relationship, and all the self-doubt that had ensued, and all it had taken was witnessing that one kiss to plummet her back into the depths of her own private hell.

She dressed in a T-shirt and shorts and immersed herself in the weight room that had served as a guest room at times. It was usually helpful when she wanted to relieve some stress and dispel the anger that usually accompanied her reminiscences about her relationship with Rick. A flat stomach and tight glutes were the best revenge and healthier than binge drinking, she thought with a smirk as she pressed her feet onto the bench press. Silently, she thanked Rick's friend for donating his old gym equipment. Who knew she would end up being the one to reap the benefits?

Rick Boutwell had been entranced with her, and she with him when she had first called on his establishment, The Galleon, as his potential liquor distributor. He had called her *The Firefly Lady* and seemed to be glad when she popped in to sell him her products. He took advantage of her promotions in the restaurant he managed, and then he began asking her out to dinner. She enjoyed the attention and the way he spent money on her. He liked her spunkiness and sharp business skills. They had been crazy about each other in the early days, and he had taken her to the bartenders' ball in Charlotte and then to a foodie show in Las Vegas, where they had gotten married on an impulse and a bottle of tequila. They had developed such an appetite for each other in those first days, and she had joked that he was like a race horse with her, barely out of the gate and across the finish line before she could even get started. At first, she had been flattered by his demands.

But then the relationship changed into something she had never expected. He stopped kissing her gently after awhile, and he became more and more demanding and rough. He never referred to having sex with her as making love; he turned it into something vulgar and impersonal. At times she didn't want it, but he always had his way in the end, and she would close her eyes and pretend he was someone else, anyone else. She used to think at those times that she knew what rape must feel like.

At parties after the restaurant closed, they would drink and he would use cocaine with his buddies. She did too sometimes. It took the edge off the bad feelings, and the way he had started to ignore her. She thought their problems had been her fault so she tried to change things, but she found she couldn't, finally realizing she was trapped in a loveless marriage. All her life she had dreamed of having a family, so she had been disappointed by her reality. After Rick had been so relieved when she had a miscarriage, she knew things would never be right between the two of them. She fell into herself and became someone she no longer recognized, cutting herself off from all of her friends, losing her self-respect.

When they had come across the old marina that was for sale, Rick had been looking for an investment, and she fell so in love with the place that he gave in and bought it, although, declaring it was a dump, he stated that he would be looking for another property soon that would be better suited to his needs. She came to love the restaurant so she quit her job with the liquor distributor, helping him envision and manage The Sound Side. He soon grew tired of the business and spent more time away from the place than there; then one day, he announced that he had found another restaurant to start, called Pompano's, so she could have her little hole in the wall if it made her happy. It was *her* place, and the more he left her alone with it, the more confident she felt taking care of the food, the staff, and the customers, creating the kind of ambience she knew was there. She immersed herself in the business and made staff changes until she had just the right combination of food, people, music, and atmosphere. It became her haven, and when the marriage fell apart, Rick had been glad to unload it on her. Her father gave her the money to buy him out, and Rick had given her the house in the divorce settlement. He was living with Torie by then anyway, so he had no desire to keep any claim to the modest beach house in Duck. Money had never been a problem with him or his family; they indulged him to do whatever his heart desired. Thankfully, he had wanted nothing to do with her anymore. But failure had still been a bitter pill for her to swallow.

The taco dinner at Shelly's house that evening was more fun than she'd expected, and she enjoyed watching the band play on Kyle's Skype set-up. She got to talk to Chelsea, and Shelly got to see Tom and Liz again. They made plans for the band to play during Kyle's last weekend there, Chelsea's birthday, and between their two houses, everyone should have a bed or some place to sleep. It would be like camp, and they would have an oyster roast on the beach. It was going to be a blast.

Kyle walked her out to her car after she had given Shelly a hug. His hands were casually in his pockets as he waited for her to say something. "So how was the surfing?" she asked at last.

He chuckled, "Brutal. Look at this," he said, twisting his arm around so she could see a large scrape on the back of it. "That's what the floor of the ocean does to a guy," he laughed. "And here, too," he said, lifting his shirt and showing her another big scrape on his side.

She felt a wave of sadness wash over her, thinking of Tyson's words. *Even when she drags you down, hard across the floor of the sea, you just get back up and do it again, waiting for that big wave that makes it all worth it.* "I don't guess that's so much fun," she sighed.

"Yeah, but it was worth it today," he said, grinning at her.

She raised her eyebrows at him and then asked him, "Hey, will you come by my place tomorrow and help me board up my windows…after we finish at the restaurant?"

"Sure, I'll come. Tyson's going to do it. But if you need me I'll come."

"I hate asking him," she mumbled, her head down.

"God, you're being such a pussy about this. Just get over it."

She gasped incredulously but playfully shoved him. He shoved her back and they pushed each other back and forth to her car, and she was hugging him. "Do you think he's really mad at me?"

"Are you kidding? He'll always give you a second chance. That's what you do when you love someone. You're so lame."

She thought about it for a minute and then nodded at him in the cloudy darkness. "All right. I'll see you at first light, 'kay?"

"'Kay," he said and bumped her knuckles with his own. "Sleep, okay? You look like shit."

She was not the first to arrive at first light at The Sound Side. Sanders and Tyson were already there, lifting the picnic tables and bringing them inside, off the deck, as Kyle and Darius, another member of the usual breakfast crew, were battening down the windows, sliding boards across the old shutters. She began carrying the front porch rockers inside. The wind had kicked up during the night, and her hair blew about her face, despite the tight bun she had tied it in. She wore a faded pink *The Sound Side* T-shirt and old shorts with a pair of beach sandals that were made for getting wet. Tyson followed her into the kitchen where they did a quick inventory of the contents of the walk-in refrigerator.

"Maybe we should put everything that freezes well into the freezer, in case we lose power," suggested Tyson; she nodded in agreement. "It will stay colder longer, and you don't want to lose any more food than you have to."

"Right, good thinking," she said. They set about moving some of the fish and the cheesecakes and her key lime pies into the freezer. Stacie was shivering after a few minutes. They took care not to bump into each other, and he held the doors for her when she had her arms full. She went to the office to pack up her laptop and met him in front of the restaurant. He held a large container out to her. "Cape May clam chowder. If you can't heat it up, you can put it in your freezer at home," he said softly. He put it in a brown paper bag with handles, the kind they gave their customers to transport their leftovers.

When she said, "Thanks," he almost smiled at her. Kyle and the others appeared at the door.

"The wind's a bitch out there. This thing's coming in faster than they said," Sanders stated, repositioning his ball cap so the brim went down the back. "I think we're all set. You need anything else, Stace?"

"No, I think we're good, guys. Y'all go on ahead…and be safe! Thanks again," she said as Sanders and Darius waved and were out the front door.

"Okay. Why don't you go on ahead and I'll board up the door behind you," said Tyson to Stacie and Kyle.

"Right, right. I'm outta here," Kyle said quickly, shooting a look at Stacie.

"Aren't you coming to my house?" she asked him in a panic.

"Why? Tyson's got it," he said giving her a ghost of a smile. She glared at him.

"You need your windows boarded up?" Tyson asked. "Sure, I've got it. You go on, Kyle. Your mom's place, okay?"

"Yeah, we're inland and it's just a Category 2. We should be good."

"All right, then. Take care, man. See you after the storm. We'll call you," Tyson nodded at him, but Kyle was already striding across the parking lot to his smoke-colored Jeep Wrangler, jingling his keys.

Stacie rolled her eyes as she locked the deadbolt to the front doors and Tyson began nailing boards in place over the doors. "Here, can you hold this?" he grunted, the muscles in his tanned arms bulging as he held a board in place. She grasped it firmly as he banged a nail in with three whacks of his hammer, and repeated the process at each corner of the board. "After this storm, I'm building you some damn door battens," he grumbled, with nails between his teeth. The job was finished and they fought the wind to their cars. He held the door for her and handed her the bag of chowder as she situated herself in her driver's seat, rubbing prickly chill bumps up and down her arms.

When they got back to her house, the sky was angry-looking and the wind was howling around the corner of her stairs as they pulled the boards out of the shed under the house and carried them upstairs. He got the ladder next and she held it for him as he climbed up to each window. She handed him the boards one by one, as the rain started to spit at them. He nailed them into place efficiently, although the rain was slashing them in sheets by the time they were done. He dragged the ladder inside the house as they set her computer and the chowder inside the kitchen door; she kicked off her wet sandals and he his wet deck shoes. A pool of water dripped off of them as they stood, breathing hard inside the dark house. The wind screamed outside.

"I am not going back out there again!" he declared, finally smiling at her, showing the dimples in his cheeks and laughing, shaking water from his wet black hair, which curled again in response.

"No," she laughed as she noticed blood dripping from his thumb. "Oh, you're bleeding," she said. They went to the sink where he ran cold water over his thumb and she opened the cabinet, reaching for her box of band-aids. She shivered, aware of how wet she was, as she pressed a paper towel tightly around his thumb and held it there. His arm felt warm next to hers.

"You're freezing," he said. "We should put that chowder on the stove before the power goes. That'll warm you up."

"Yeah, it's the AC too. We should get into some dry clothes."

"I have some here, right?" he said, looking directly at her for the first time in days.

"Yeah, I think so. In your drawer. I washed clothes yesterday," she said, shaking as she moved the paper towel and applied the band-aid to his thumb.

"Thanks. Good as new."

"Thanks for helping me. It sucks being alone."

He looked at her again and sighed. "I know."

She went to get the container of chowder as he pulled a pot out from the cabinet beside the stove. It was comforting working together again in her kitchen as they had done for so many months. She poured some of the chowder into the pot and stowed the rest in the fridge as he went to adjust the thermostat, watching her shivering again. She laughed, embarrassed.

They went into the bedroom and pulled open drawers, reaching for dry clothes. As Tyson peeled off his wet shirt and dropped it on the floor, she tried not to stare at his toned and tanned torso. She noticed a little rivulet of water flow from his large wet black curls on the back of his neck. She saw the tattoo on his bicep, the ring of thorns, and looked at his chest, but then she had to look away as he stripped the rest of his clothes off and dropped them as well on the floor.

"What? I'll pick them up," he said, misreading her eyes completely.

She pretended nonchalance and began peeling herself out of her own wet clothes, leaving a pile beside his. She got to her bra and panties and hesitated.

"So, you're modest now?" he said seriously, holding his clothes, looking at her with raised brows. She thought he might laugh at her, but he did not. She unhooked the bra and let it fall, then peeled off her wet lavender panties that she remembered were his favorite, and stood shivering. He jerked the covers back from her bed and said, "Get in." His hot green eyes were large as he gazed at her; she knew, cold as she was, he was getting a show.

"Damn, Stacie, your lips are blue. Get in the bed," he commanded impatiently. She did. He slid on a pair of blue boxers and slipped in beside her, sighing and sliding his arm under her head, cradling it and stroking her wet hair and her face with his hand. He rubbed her arm, her back, her hip, and her leg with his other hand. "This is the best way to get you warm right now," he said into her ear.

She shivered again, closed her eyes, and let him take care of her. She felt his lips press against her forehead as he continued to stroke her face, pulling it close to his. Finally, she let herself wrap her arms around him and fold into his warmth. He was silent, and when she allowed herself to gaze up at him, his eyes were closed. She sighed. "I hate it when you don't smile at me anymore. I guess that's my fault." She felt a huge sob forming in her throat. She couldn't remember the last time she had cried. "I'm so sorry I ever doubted you," she said. Large hot tears began to roll down her face. He opened his eyes and wiped her tears with his hand.

"This was never about me, was it?" he whispered, looking deep into her eyes. She shook her head. "What did he do to you, Stace?" he asked, holding her tightly into him. She let herself weep into his neck as he held her wordlessly, kissing and stroking her.

"I'm sorry," she said over and over as he tried to quiet her crying.

"It's okay. All that is over. It's just us now. Forget him," he murmured into her face, soothing her as he slid his hands over her shoulders, onto her breasts, and down her body gently. He kissed her passionately, and she took his mouth in hers with the same burning longing. They began to make love as the rain pounded on her roof and the wind roared around them.

The power went out as predicted. He brought her warm chowder that they ate by candlelight. He found the Tiffany box on the bedside table and slid the sparkling ring back onto her finger, warning her never to take it off again. It was impossible to sleep. They snuggled under the soft covers of the bed and listened to the storm raging around them, wondering whether the cars would be washed away; for a time, Stacie felt her heart racing with the sound of the storm outside.

Tyson held her face up to look into her eyes and asked, "Why didn't you tell me?"

"About what?" she asked, confused.

"You went to the doctor, right? That day when I was in your office, I saw it written on your calendar, and then, we never got a chance to talk about it. What did she say?"

Stacie was quiet a moment; then suddenly, she felt a returning ray of the hope she had known that day, before things had become so convoluted and disorienting. "I need to have another surgery. She said there's a very small chance I could have a baby, after that, if we're careful. I'd have to cut back on my hours and maybe delegate some responsibilities, but it could happen. The other alternative would be to go ahead with the hysterectomy…."

He nodded. "That was what you'd decided, wasn't it?" he asked gravely, meeting her gaze.

"Maybe, yeah, for a few days, that's what I thought I should do. What do *you* want?" she asked him earnestly.

"Baby, it's not about me…."

"Yes it is. You're in this too. You have to tell me if you don't want this."

"I just want you to be healthy. You're all that matters. If we had kids…a child, I would be really happy, but it's not the most important thing. We'd be really good parents. I know that. That's what you want, right?"

"You know, it was always what I wanted, but I'm okay with whatever happens. I just want you. I don't ever want to lose you again."

"You never lost me," he said, amused. "Remember that story about the ocean? I told you I'm not going anywhere. I've waited long enough to get you where I want you," he said, sliding her on top of him and stretching himself underneath her. She sat up and looked down at him.

"On top?"

"Yeah. I like a woman who can hold her own on top," he said, cupping his hands around her hips and looking up at her, smiling. "Besides, the view from down here is the most beautiful thing I've ever seen." She leaned forward and kissed him, running her hand along the side of his face.

Chapter 5

CHANGES

Stacie woke to silence, and then upon careful listening, she heard the mild rolling of waves on the beach, realizing that the storm had passed. Tyson was gone. She could not tell what time it was with the boards over the windows. Sitting up and combing her hair back away from her face, she felt rested and calm. After pulling on the clothes she had intended to wear the day before, she looked about for the wet pile they had dropped before surrendering to their bed for the storm's duration. Tyson must have put them in the laundry. Still no power, she thought as she looked at her bedside table with its blank clock face. A vague spraying sound was barely audible as she slipped on flip-flops and opened the front door, feeling warm sun hit her pleasantly. Tyson was below the house, spraying the salt water off their cars with the hose. "They didn't wash away after all!" he called up to her, grinning, and squinting into the sunlight.

"How long have you been up?" she asked, realizing he had put the hammock back up and carried the rocking chairs back out onto the porch.

"Not long. I didn't want to wake you," he said, climbing the stairs. "You needed the rest," he said, kissing her, and wiping his hands on his shorts. Seeing the gray T-shirt he wore stretched tightly across his chest, she took in a breath, remembering last night and why she would have been so tired.

"I have blueberry scones and iced tea for breakfast. Aren't you starving?" she asked him, putting her arm around his waist and pulling him into a hug.

"Starvin' for you," he murmured into her ear, returning her hug. Then he cast his eyes about the porch and her property. "There wasn't that much damage…not like what I thought it would be from the sound of things last night. We can take these boards down in a bit and ride over to The Sound Side if you want."

"Do you think the power's out all over the island?"

"Probably," he said. "Maybe you'll get another day off out of it. You need a break."

"I'd kill for a cup of coffee," she said hoarsely.

"Lucky for you I brought my propane stove," he grinned, gesturing in the doorway at a box he was already starting to unpack. "How does an omelet sound, ma'am?"

She shook her head. "You're amazing."

"Just prepared," he said modestly.

They walked on the shell-littered beach after checking on the restaurant which seemed no worse for the wear, and then called their families to let everyone know they were safe. Stacie talked to Shelly and Kyle, and then called Bets and Lucy to let them know everything was fine. They discussed the upcoming beach party that was in the works for the last weekend in July, just days before Kyle's departure for UVA and football practice. Tyson decided to invite his family down from the Jersey shore as well. It would be the perfect time for their families to meet and celebrate their engagement together, and maybe nail down some plans in the process. They could close the restaurant on Thursday for a private party, and the weekend would be dedicated to introducing everyone to their families and enjoying the new band.

They took cold showers in the outdoor shower, and then they drove down to Tyson's place to check on his duplex. It was easier taking down his battens, as he had devised and installed channels on the tops and bottoms of each window, so all they had to do was slide the boards out and stow them in his shed. As they climbed the stairs to his place, he warned her, "I didn't clean. Don't be too horrified."

She was not horrified and hardly surprised at the mess inside. She had seen it before, the stacks of books, scattered here and there, some lying open on the floor and some with papers shoved inside as markers. The kitchen was immaculate; she remembered that his cookware and knives were nicer than what she allowed herself to possess at her own home. "I know…I'm a slob. This is *so* not up to your standards," he apologized, running his hand through his dark curls that were almost dry from the shower at her place. His power was not on either, and by now the sun was streaming in the windows and the lack of air conditioning made for a stuffy atmosphere. He cracked a window for relief. She suggested that he pack some clothes and they head back up to her place, as she took in his unmade bed and the pile of laundry on top of his washer that she could see in the open closet next to his kitchen.

She excused herself to his bathroom and after washing her hands, on an impulse, slid back the shower curtain to inspect the tub shower, which was surprisingly clean.

"I'm a slob, not a pig," he smirked when she emerged from the bathroom. "There's a difference. I heard you snooping around in there," he added and she laughed, caught in her act. "I've been around you too long ever to let it get bad. Never know when you'll show up and need the facilities…a guy's gotta put his best foot forward," he said, a slow smile spreading across his face, forming dimples at each end that took her breath away. When he slid his hand along her jaw and pulled her face into his for the sweetest of kisses, she melted into him, landing them both on the unmade bed.

"You know, it would only take you about ten minutes to pack all this stuff up and bring it up to Duck for good."

"You mean to *your* place? You're just after my *cookware*," he whispered, sliding his hand into her camisole top and finding her breast.

"No. I'm totally serious…and besides it's not really my place. It belongs to National City Mortgage, if you're getting technical." She was having difficulty speaking as his kisses took over the function of her mouth for the moment.

He pulled away and his sultry green eyes looked into hers for a long moment. "How much is your mortgage payment?"

She told him, and he laughed, "Why didn't I ever think of that? If I paid you my half as rent, my dick status would be revoked."

"Exactly," she murmured into his neck, close to his ear. "Throw in that cookware…and the knives…and the propane stove and I think we have a deal."

"*Deal*," he moaned, unbuttoning the waistband of her cargo Capris.

They reopened The Sound Side on Wednesday. Stacie had spent her free time on Tuesday looking over the bartender applications she had received for a part-time female. Most of the applicants were looking for full-time work, or at least more hours than she could promise, except for one person, Ava Beckley, age twenty-five, who lived at a temporary address in Kill Devil Hills. Stacie had called Ava and set up an interview for 3:30 p.m. today.

Stacie arrived at 3 o'clock, dressed in her dinner attire, which was always different from her casual dress during breakfast and lunch. This afternoon, she wore her midnight blue birthday dress and the sea glass earrings. Her sun-bleached blonde hair was long and loose, and she was fresh from a shower and a good night's sleep, knowing Tyson would finally be with her every night, as a permanent resident in their home, which made life all the sweeter in her mind.

Ava sat alone at the bar, empty now, due to the time of day, drinking from her personal bottle of spring water, wearing jeans and a simple, white halter top. She was dark-haired and willowy, making eye contact while immediately flashing a brief but pleasant smile. Stacie thought she looked like the perfect person for the job, if her references could stand the test.

"Hi, Ava, I'm Stacie Edmonds," she said warmly, extending her hand.

"Hi, Stacie," Ava smiled, handing Stacie the application form she'd completed.

Stacie thanked her, looking over it carefully. "May I see your driver's license?" she asked. She cross-referenced Ava's application with the license to make sure the birthdates matched. The I.D. looked real. Stacie swallowed calmly and slowed the interaction until she felt in control of the situation. Ava looked at her with a frank expression and sipped from her water bottle. It was indeed a hot day.

"So, tell me…why are you looking for a job now? It's a little late in the summer just to be striking out."

"My family just got here," Ava said, a smile beginning on her full lips, green-brown eyes meeting Stacie's playfully. "I'm a nanny and we've been traveling. We just landed here before the Fourth of July…and then Abigail hit. I'm just looking for something part-time," she smiled.

"You're a nanny?"

"Yes, I take care of two girls and a boy between the ages of six and eleven for a doctor's family here in Kill Devil Hills."

"Oh. Where were you before this?"

"New York. The kids' grandmother lives in Manhattan, but they have a summer home here and we just arrived, as I said," she said indulgently.

"Do you do this job all year?"

"No, just during the summers. I live in Charlotte year round. I teach Spanish at Independence High School."

"Really? I'm from Charlotte. Where in Charlotte do you live?"

She smiled, "Elizabeth. Do you know it?"

Stacie smiled at her. "Yes, small world...where did you go to college?"

"I went to ECU. I spent some time abroad after that, working on the language."

"East Carolina University...I got my marketing degree there. Real small world," commented Stacie, nodding to herself. This girl was looking good. "So where did you learn to bartend?"

Ava smiled and looked down at her unmanicured hands. "Actually I learned in Barcelona. I wasn't really good at Spanish then, so I may have gotten some of the orders wrong...but it was loads of fun. I really didn't care!"

Stacie laughed and stood up. "Well, come on back here. Let's see what you can do." She watched as Ava walked around behind the bar, inspecting all the bottles of liquor and the wine racks. She was definitely as tall as Stacie had assessed from her seat.

Her eyes flickered to the refrigerator and she asked, "May I?" as Stacie nodded. She opened the door and appeared to be assessing the mixers and garnishes left over from the last evening's service. "So, what'll it be, miss?"

"Score one for Ava!" Stacie laughed, referring to the "miss." "Chick drink or guy drink?"

"Oh, let's do a chick drink…they're way more involved. How about the rave on the beach, at least I *think*. I haven't been here very long! A mojito?"

"Sure," Stacie said. Ava set to looking around the bar, reaching into the fridge and pulling out mint leaves and limes, taking a tall narrow glass and mashing mint and limes carefully, all the while asking Stacie questions.

"How long have you had this place?"

"It's been mine a little over three years."

"I've been in here before. I love the bands. There's a guy that plays by himself every so often…I think he bartends here too."

"Andrew?"

"Dark hair? Brooding good looks? Unbelievable smile?" she smiled herself, pouring in rum and seltzer.

Stacie grinned, "He's the one. You sound like a fan."

"In the *worst* way. Would that be a problem…if he works here?"

"I don't know. That would be up to you."

She shrugged. "No…I think I have pretty high moral standards…after all I teach high school and take care of three kids. I think I'm lucky to be employed at all. I'm not about to blow that! Plus, I'm actually a little shy. I like being *behind* the bar, rather than out there. It's much safer!" She laughed, sliding the mojito across the bar to Stacie. It was excellent.

"Did you make these in Barcelona?"

"All the time. I served Lance Armstrong once," she grinned.

"Wow!" Stacie couldn't help herself from saying.

Ava lowered her eyes momentarily. "I have to confess something. I've worked on this beach before…but I'd never give you the owner's name as a reference."

"Why?" Stacie felt her eyes widen in interest.

"He was just a real ass," she mumbled dismissively. "I'm sorry. I wouldn't normally say something like that. You don't even know me, but this guy was unbelievable!"

"Where did you work?"

"A place called Pompano's," Ava said. "Do you know it?"

Stacie blinked twice and then smiled broadly at her. "When can you start?"

Wednesday was Zack's night off so Stacie placed a call to Andrew, telling him he had a new person to train. She tied her hair up into a loose bun and slid her white apron over her head, tying it around her waist and humming to herself, turning on Jack Jackson on the new sound system she had bought because Tyson and Andrew had convinced her to upgrade. It was half an hour before everyone would begin to arrive for the dinner shift, and she did not yet feel like sitting behind her desk to do dreary paperwork on such a lovely day. She took a basket and wandered out into the herb garden at the side of the front porch. Tyson would need cilantro for the fish tacos on special for tonight, dill for the shrimp salad, and parsley for the crab cakes. Ava had used the last of the mint leaves in her mojito so Stacie gathered more of those as well. All of the herbs were sandy from the storm, so when she took the pile back into the kitchen, she rinsed it all thoroughly. After spreading it on paper towels, she sat at the counter in the kitchen and set about snipping the ends off the green beans she and Tyson had picked up from their favorite produce market the day before. She hummed along to the music as she heard the back door squeak open and bang shut, and then he was there, in a faded yellow T-shirt, removing his sunglasses from his dark face and smiling broadly when he saw her. She grinned back.

"Wow," he said. "This is what made me fall in love with you, seeing you here, just like this, doin' your thing." He walked behind her, kissing the back of her neck, and slipping his own apron over his head. He washed his hands at the hand sink and dried them on a paper towel. "So…did you hire a barkeep?" he asked tentatively.

She nodded. "I did. She's coming in tonight for training with Andrew. I think she'll be great. She made me a bangin' mojito. Her name is Ava. She's a nanny for a family here, and she teaches high school Spanish back in Charlotte. Believe it or not, she worked at Pompano's last summer."

"Hmm, she must not know the connection," he remarked, smiling.

"No, and I didn't tell her. I guess she'll find out soon enough. She just said that the boss was an ass," she said, eyes twinkling. Tyson regarded her warily. "At least she was up front about it. I like that in her. It reminds me of something I would have said! Anyway, none of that is an issue anymore," she said, looking into his eyes carefully.

"That's what I like to hear," he said, winking at her and noticing the herbs drying by the sink. "You've been busy, I see," he said.

"Mm-hmm, beats sitting in the office. What have you been up to?"

"I was dumping some stuff from the duplex and *cleaning*, you'll be glad to know. The fam has decided to stay there when they all come down in two weeks. I'll hang onto it until the first of August anyway, so we might as well get some use out of it."

"You must have talked to them today? Did you tell them you moved in up here?" she asked, wording it diplomatically.

"Yeah, my mother can't wait to see you again. She's really excited about coming down. Since she retired from teaching, she's been all about some traveling."

"That's great for them. And your dad won't have any trouble leaving his boat business? I would think the summer is his busiest time, like it is for us."

"It is, but he has really good people working for him, so he can afford to be gone for a few days. He doesn't do it often. You know, it will be really good seeing them all again. It's been since…I don't know when we've all been together. I guess since Jesse and Mel's wedding a couple of years ago….Anyway, I can't believe they're all coming."

"I hope the weather will be good."

Another squeaking and banging of the back door announced more staff arriving; this time it was Nina, followed in the next moment by Kyle. His face lit up distinctly when he saw the two of them looking so comfortable. After saying hello, Kyle and Nina started pulling out butter and sour cream from the walk-in as Tyson mixed crabmeat with breadcrumbs, eggs, green pepper, onions, and parsley he had just chopped.

At five, Andrew arrived to get the lowdown on the new bartender. Stacie was careful not to mention that Ava was a fan of his. He was much too self-effacing to deal with it just yet, and she doubted Ava would mention it yet either. It would be interesting to watch the two shy lovelies interact tonight. Nina scolded her later, hearing about it, as they sat in the dining room, wrapping silverware in soft paper napkins.

"Always the matchmaker!" she laughed and shook her head, thinking about how her own union with Zack was a result of Stacie's intervention.

"Nonsense! All I have to do is put the right people in the right places. The rest is in God's hands! I don't do a thing!" Stacie laughed.

"Well, I'm just glad you got yours. It took you and Tyson long enough. But, seriously, I'm so glad for you guys that it's worked out for you. You're so right for each other. Poor Andrew. He won't know what hit him!"

"We'll see. Lucky for her, he's playing next weekend."

"Don't we have some kind of non-fraternization policy?"

"I should. I *had* to say that to all those Mary Washington girls last year when they were all over my baby nephew," she laughed, remembering the frenzy that Alex, Kate, and Lilia had all worked themselves into over Kyle. Not that the policy had sunk in with Kate after two summers on her staff, she thought to herself.

Nina giggled, tucking escaped blonde curls back into her ponytail. "I remember your screaming, '*He's jailbait!*' to all of them last summer. God, it was so funny the way they *wanted* him!"

"Well, he was in no shape to be dealing with all of that then. He was so lucky to find Chelsea. And see? I had nothing to do with that. It's just fate, like I said."

"Yeah, God has a way of looking out for us, even when we don't ask."

And *especially when we do*, Stacie thought, as the first party of four walked through the front door. She picked up menus, and after greeting them, led them to a table overlooking the sound. Nina prepared to greet them as Ava walked in the front door, in a black sleeveless top, black pants, and comfortable shoes. Stacie introduced her to Andrew, who shook her hand politely and began to show her around the bar. He then guided her through the computer program, teaching her how to clock in and enter her orders. Stacie went back to the kitchen to check on the dinner preparations as cooks, dish people, and servers buzzed about efficiently, laughing and talking, under Tyson's direction. Knowing everything was under control, she forced herself into the office, flipping on the lamp, to prepare next week's food order. An hour later, she was watching the paper go through the fax machine when Andrew appeared at the doorway.

"Hi," she smiled, looking up at him from her paisley reading glasses. "Is everything okay? How's Ava working out?"

He chuckled softly and leaned into the doorframe. "Stellar, actually. I came to ask whether she can just stay the rest of the night. She's doing great and we're starting to get busy already. It will give you a break, so…" he said, shrugging slightly.

As her slow smile began to creep across her face, he frowned at her.

"What?" he asked, shifting his weight in the doorway, glancing behind him.

"Nothing. I knew I'd found a good one is all. If she can stay, tell her we'll be glad to have her till closing." She took off the glasses and twisted a strand of hair around her finger as he continued to eye her suspiciously.

"Cool. Thanks," he said warily; he watched her an extra moment before he turned to walk back to the bar. She sat back in her chair and stretched her arms over her head. It felt so good to be back in the groove again.

Chapter 6

MORE CHANGES

The families and the band were set to arrive on the last Thursday of July. Stacie, Tyson, Shelly, and Kyle had set about massive house cleaning efforts in preparation for the guests' arrival. Extra seafood had been ordered for the oyster roast and low country boil that would be in store for a private party at The Sound Side on Thursday evening, and an off-shore fishing trip had been chartered for all the interested men for Sunday when the restaurant was closed. Stacie had planned to host a brunch at her house that day for the ladies so they could relax at the beach. A beach bonfire and hot dog roast would be the highlight on Sunday night after the fishermen returned. Everyone would be leaving on Monday morning and life at the beach would resume…hectic, at best, and hopefully with some wedding plans in place.

Stacie wandered into the office on Wednesday. She had just returned from a visit to the chapel by the sea in Nags Head to see whether it would be possible to hold a marriage ceremony there. She found Tyson seated at her desk. In the lamplight, he looked scholarly in a collared shirt and her purple glasses peering at her computer screen.

"Cute," she commented, grinning at him. "What are you doing?"

He smirked and removed the readers. "Checking my stocks and mutual funds," he said, his eyes taking in her floral print skirt, sleeveless top, and hair pulled into a loose bun. His eyes softened. "You look nice. What did you find out?"

"Well, since we were both raised in the Episcopal Church, we can get married there. Father Jack is a real hoot. He says they have a date open the third weekend in October…and then there's January, but who wants that, right? And since I've been divorced, I need special permission from the bishop, but after we talk again, he'll send in a letter and ask for approval. He didn't have a lot of time, so we're planning to talk in a couple of weeks." She noticed his hands were in his lap, his left wrapped around his right. She took a step toward him and peeked over the desk at his hands. "What's wrong with your hand?" she asked.

He held it up, setting a zip-lock bag of crushed ice onto the desk in the process. "Hmm. It seems it had a run in with some asshole's face down at the boat dock."

She looked horrified. "What? Did you get into a fight? What happened?"

"It wasn't a fight, really. I just had to deck somebody," he said, taking off the glasses and tossing them on her desk. "Oh, I guess you'll hear about it eventually. Zack and I went down to Oregon Inlet to book the fishing trip and ran into your ex. He congratulated me on my 'promotion' and I just had to smash his face, that's all."

Her mouth formed a small O and she breathed in slowly. "You were fighting with Rick in broad daylight?"

"No, like I said, I just decked him. Zack let me get in a couple of good licks and then he pulled me off him before it got out of hand. Rick's friend Chuck was there, so he pulled Rick up off the dock; that was as far as it went. Mostly there was applause. The people standing around know us and were in our corner, I guess," he shrugged.

She looked at him incredulously. "And you don't think he's going to press charges?"

"Are you kidding? He knows better. He provoked it. I was defending your honor."

"You were defending *my* honor?"

"Yeah," he said as if she were slow to comprehend. "He disrespects me, and he disrespects you. That's uncalled for, and he won't get away with any of that shit on my watch." He stood, picking up the ice pack, and stepped past her on his way out the door. "That son of a bitch knows where he stands now," he muttered, tossing the bag of ice into the trashcan before going into the kitchen to begin his dinner preparations.

Stacie shook her head and set her yellow purse on the desk, picking up the glasses absently and twirling them around in her hand. She wondered what Father Jack would make of all of this! She was sure the poor priest had no idea of the mess he was about to clean up, marrying the two of them! She sat down in the chair and adjusted her bra, which felt tight and sticky in the July humidity. A laugh escaped her lips, and then she let it peal forth freely, imagining the scene, wondering how long it would take Zack to come in to tell her about the whole scenario, considering it was his day off, and she would not see him until the party tomorrow night, most likely. By then it was sure to be a good story with his usual embellishments. Rick's antics had always been a favorite subject with him as well. With Tyson in *her* corner, she was sure to be well taken care of for the rest of her life, and the thought of it gave her a serene sense of pleasure.

She went to find him in the kitchen. He was standing in the walk-in refrigerator, opening boxes of produce that had been delivered earlier in the day. Going to him, she took his right hand, raising it to her lips and kissing his knuckles, still cool from the ice, pressing the back of it to her face, meeting his eyes with a mixture of amusement and admiration.

He smiled at her. "You're *my* baby now. I'm not letting anything happen to you…ever again," he murmured into her ear and wrapped her into his warm embrace.

That night after Stacie had taken her turn in the bathroom, she padded into the moonlit bedroom in her bathrobe and bare feet, hair up and damp around the ends from washing her face. Tyson was sprawled, naked and prone across the bed, with arms raised above his head, his usual silent request for a well deserved back rub after a long night in the kitchen. She rubbed lotion into her hands and sat beside him on the bed. "You must be whipped," she commented. "We were slammed all night. I know we have to work like dogs in the summer to make it all year, but sometimes, don't you wonder if it's all worth it?"

He groaned in response and she giggled, sliding the palm of her hand along the suppleness of his lower back. He moaned again and she added her other hand to work in synchrony on the other side. Her fingertips worked their way out to the broad curves of his shoulders and over to the center, meeting at his neck and descending again, all the way to his buttocks and then back again in slow deliberate sequences.

"Don't get too comfortable, cowboy," she warned softly. "I get mine too, later."

"Oh, you'll get yours, don't worry," he whispered against the sheets, his eyes mere slits directed her way.

His skin was soft and smooth from salt water and summer sweat; she liked the feel of it beneath her fingers. She climbed onto his back and continued her massage, feeling the heavy rise and fall of his breathing, thinking he had fallen asleep under her touch. Then, he rolled over. His sleepy green eyes opened as he slowly untied her robe and opened it. She pulled it off the rest of the way and draped it over the end of the bed, loosening her hair and letting it fall to one side. When she looked back at him, he was gazing poignantly at her, eyes wide and questioning.

"What is it?" she asked him, gently, letting her hands rest on his stomach.

"Mmm," he said, barely audibly. "There's nothing more beautiful than a pregnant woman," he said, eyes smiling into hers.

She caught her breath. She supposed she should have known, but had somehow let herself slip into that safe, dreamlike cocoon of denial she was so good at seeking out in the past. It had been over thirty days since her last period, and she had abandoned the pack of pills in her bathroom drawer, figuring her body was so out of whack that it would happen when it would happen. It had to have been those disconcerting days and the day of the storm when she had forgotten to take them. Still, she stared at him with large blue eyes; he appeared to be amused, moving his hands tenderly up and down her legs, and spreading his fingers across her belly.

"Didn't you know?" he laughed gently. "Or were you planning on surprising me?"

"How...how do *you* know?"

He cupped his hands softly around her breasts. "These are heavier..." he said and circled his thumbs around the areolas of her nipples. "And these are bigger and darker," he said, shifting her off of him so she could lie beside him. He traced his finger in a line from her navel down a few inches, and said, "In a few weeks, you'll have a dark line right about here." His fingertips continued down between her legs and felt what she already knew was happening.

"How do you know this?" she whispered as he hovered over her, leaning in to take her breast tenderly in his mouth, kissing it, then looking back into her eyes.

"I read a lot," he smiled.

"Liar," she gasped as he pushed himself gently inside her.

It was 4:15 a.m. when she emerged from the bathroom with the white stick in the pocket of her robe. He was not in the bed. Eventually, she saw him sitting out on the dune at the end of the boardwalk, a blanket wrapped around his waist. She walked outside to join him in the warm night breeze. When she was beside him, she looked over at the blanket, and tried for light humor.

"Are you naked under there?"

"Mm-hmm. Chicks dig this."

"Mmm," she laughed, raising her eyebrows a notch. "No bugs tonight," she commented, wrapping her robe around her.

"Wind's offshore. Lots of stars though. I just saw one fall." He smiled up at her, taking her hand and helping her sit down beside him on the dune.

"Did you make a wish?" she asked, settling herself next to him, feeling their shoulders touch.

"I think I got my wish already," he said, looking straight ahead, but then glancing at her sideways.

"I just did a test," she announced. "There's a little pink plus sign in the box. I guess we're pregnant after all." He said nothing, but she saw a smile form at the corners of his mouth from her sideways glance. After a quiet moment, she cleared her throat and said, "So…I guess I need to know how my fiancé knows how beautiful, naked, pregnant women look." She spoke as if it were a question and looked directly at him, resting her cheek on her arms that she had folded around her knees. He dropped his eyes to the blanket between his knees. When he was silent for too long, she laughed. "Don't tell me there's a little Tyson junior walking around Cape May or New York…or Florida somewhere?"

He shook his head and laughed silently. "No, nothing like that."

"So?"

He took a deep breath and let it out slowly. "When I was a senior at Columbia, my girlfriend got pregnant. She was a promising art student who was getting her MFA there when I came along."

"Ah, another older woman."

"Not by much. Her parents were outraged, of course, but it was way more than just that. They were an FFV—First Family of Virginia—and I was just this bum from New Jersey."

"They obviously didn't know you."

"Well, her dad was some hot shot intelligence guy in McLean. Jamie was supposed to be going to study in Europe, but then she dropped the bomb on them..." he shrugged and shook his head.

"What happened? Did she have an abortion?"

"No. *They* wanted her to end the pregnancy. But she wanted to have the baby. It made them crazy. She talked about giving it up for adoption. She talked about getting married, but she really didn't know what she wanted. Apparently it wasn't me," he said dejectedly. "They thought I was putting weird ideas into her head. Her father was a very compelling man and pretty much had her realizing she didn't need me in her life." He got quiet again.

"But you wanted the baby?"

"It was up to her. I would have married her if she'd wanted me."

"You loved her that much?"

"Yeah, I did. Of course, that was before I knew you and all of this we have between us. What did I know back then? Her parents hated me and didn't want me near her from the beginning, and then that happened. I've never been the target of such hatred. Not in my family, not with anyone

I've ever known. I'm not the type to piss anybody off…at least not until *today* maybe. Anyway, she was going home at Christmas break. I was going to wait and see what she decided to do. I thought I'd never see her again. I figured they wouldn't let her come back after the holidays. But she never made it home. She hit a patch of black ice on the way home that night and lost control of her car. It went down an embankment…and she died," he said quietly, as if reliving it yet again. "She'd gotten all the way to McLean, so it happened not far from her house."

Stacie stared at him. How awful for him, first to be dumped, and then to lose the one you loved! Stacie's breath caught in her throat as she started to speak. She had to swallow to get out the words. "I'm so sorry…I had no idea."

"I know. It was so…*bad*. Her father called me and told me about it. He was livid with me, like I had caused it. He told me I wasn't welcome at her funeral."

"You went anyway, didn't you?"

He smiled ruefully. "I couldn't *not* go. It would have gone against everything I believed about her. I wasn't trying to go against their wishes, but it was about her and me, not them. I laid a red rose on her casket. I think her mom was over it by then…she got it, but I could tell her father still hated me. We didn't even speak. I don't know…I couldn't really blame him. I'd probably feel the same way if some asshole knocked up my daughter."

"And that was why you didn't graduate," she murmured, remembering when she'd met him that he'd said he was one semester shy of a history degree.

"I tried to. I went back to school. But I couldn't concentrate. I was failing most of my classes by mid-semester. So I went home. My mom's friend needed help at her inn in the kitchen so I got into it and decided I liked cooking. It was something I was good at. It was busy and therapeutic in a way. I could finally sleep. I couldn't stay in Cape May, though. It was too much. My parents were so worried about me and so disappointed, even though they tried not to show it. The plan was always for me to go to law school and be something special."

She circled her arm around his shoulders and pulled his face closer to hers. "You *are*...so special. You're the most wonderful person I've ever met. You can do anything you want to do. If you still want to go back to school you should do it."

When he smiled, she knew what he was thinking, *Yeah, right, with a baby on the way and a restaurant to run full tilt.* "No, it's fine. It's working out the way it's supposed to. It's a good thing I was so adrift. I came here searching for waves and I found you," he said, looking at her suddenly.

She smiled and kissed him, then sighed and said morosely, "Oh, God, Ty, what are we thinking? We don't even have time to take care of a *cat*."

He laughed and rubbed her knee, pulling it into his own. "It will be fine. I've got everything I want. Do you? Are you happy about this?"

"Yes," she said definitely, looking at him directly. "I love you so much."

"I love you, too. We'll make it work. You really don't have to be at the restaurant all the time, you know. You have good people. You don't have to kill yourself."

She gazed at him for a moment and then asked, "Why didn't you tell me all this before? When Kyle and Shelly were here at spring break, and she told him about Desiree's abortion before she died, you could have brought it up then...."

"No. That was your family's deal. You didn't need another take on any of that. Kyle didn't need to know it. I don't think he needs to know it now."

She sighed again. "I don't think I'm ready to talk to any of them about this, or the pregnancy right now. I'd like to see Dr. Walters again before we break the news to our families."

"Sure. That's understandable. I'll do whatever you want. Do you want me to go to the doctor with you?"

She threaded her fingers in his hair, touched by his offer. "I'd like that. She'd like to see you again, too." He leaned toward her and kissed her gently, their lips cool from the breeze. "And I guess we'd better try to get some sleep. I have to be up in an hour for breakfast."

He chuckled. "Can I make a request as your fiancé and the father of your child? *Get rid of breakfast!*"

"Oh, I'm there, believe me. When Sanders and Darius go back to school in the fall, breakfast at The Sound Side will be history."

Chelsea knocked on the door at 3:30 p.m. Stacie was there in an instant to greet her, her brother Jay, and his college friends who together formed her band for the weekend. They would be collectively bunking at her house, while Chelsea and her parents were staying with Shelly and Kyle for the long weekend.

"Hi, sweetheart! And happy birthday!" Stacie sang out to now eighteen-year-old Chelsea as she opened the front door to hug her young friend who looked as radiant as ever. "Jay, hi, it's good to see you again," she said and hugged Chelsea's brother, whom she had met at Chelsea and Kyle's graduation in early June.

Jay ran a hand through his tangle of blonde hair and opened his brown eyes wide, grinning at Stacie. "Hey, Stacie! Thanks for having us. This is Lauren, and Emily, and Vanessa," he said, introducing a blonde, a ginger-haired girl, and a dark brunette, all of whom Stacie thought were equally beautiful as they each greeted her and shook her hand politely. "And this is Sam, and Les," he said, rounding out the group, ushering in a slight fellow with light brown hair and a clipped beard, and a large, bear-like man with wire-framed glasses and long sandy hair tied back in a pony tail. They carried considerably little luggage upstairs with them. She showed them to their rooms, where the girls would be occupying the beds and the boys would be drawing straws over the pull-out couch and an air mattress on the living room floor.

Stacie held up her hands in defense and said, "I know, you're all adults and what goes on in the house stays in the house, just as long as I don't hear anything too crazy!" After they laughed, she showed them where to find towels and washcloths and then took them on a tour of the bathroom and the outdoor shower, which they all pronounced to be awesome. As they settled themselves in, Chelsea slid her arm around Stacie's waist.

"This is so great of you to let them stay here, and play at The Sound Side too. I think all they care about is if the toilet flushes, you know? They just want to spend time at the beach and see the island, so you probably won't see too much of them. They won't be getting in your hair."

"Sweetie, it's fine. I'll be at the restaurant most of the time on Friday and Saturday anyway. As long as they remember to lock up when they leave here, we'll be good."

"Oooh, let me see this ring! Wow, Tyson did really well! This is beautiful!" Chelsea swooned, holding Stacie's left hand up to inspect the ring she had heard about over the phone. "I'm so happy for you both!" she said, smiling. "This engagement thing is working for you. You look really great!"

"Thank you! And you too! Where is my nephew?"

"He's helping everybody get settled in at their place. My dad was breaking out the beer when I left to come over here. It's great seeing Kyle again. This will be it for a while…" she said, smiling a little sadly.

"I know. Are you getting excited about the School of the Arts?" Stacie asked, attempting to divert any sadness.

"Yes, actually I am. I met my roommate at orientation. She's from Greensboro, and I think we'll get along really well. She's a ballet dancer like me. She *hates* drama like me, too!"

"Good! You deserve a break! Tyson is down at his place, settling in his family; we'll all be meeting at the restaurant around 5:30."

"Have you met his family?"

"Just his parents. They're great. He's so much like each of his parents, in different ways. But I've yet to meet the brothers and Mel, Jesse's wife. He hasn't seen them in a long time."

"So he's moved in finally?"

"Yes. It's so much better this way."

"You look really good, really different…" Chelsea said, squinting her eyes a bit at Stacie.

When they all met at The Sound Side later in the early evening, Stacie cornered Tyson in the kitchen. "What if people notice I look different? Chelsea's already sort of picked up on it, and then, I'm not going to be drinking. They're all *bound* to notice that!" she whispered, panic in her tone.

He made a dismissive face, "Nah! All's you need is a brown bottle. I was brought up on Budweiser and Bruce Springsteen. I have a ton of Buds in the cooler out there for my dad and brothers. No one will notice if you're fake drinking out of a brown bottle. Just raise it to your lips and pretend. I'll keep one in your hand so Zack won't be tempted to make you any martinis. You should just tell him you insist he take the night off and stay out from behind the bar."

"Do I look different?" she asked him anxiously.

He tilted his head back, looked her over, and smiled. "It was a good idea not to dress so revealingly tonight. You just look beautiful as always. Just don't look like the cat that swallowed the canary!" he laughed and stroked her hair away from her cheek. "We'll make it through this. Promise."

She sighed deeply. "I didn't think I would be this nervous!"

"Don't be on my family's account!" He chuckled and checked a pot of oysters, steaming on the stove, and then the pot beside it, filled with shrimp, sausages, potatoes, and corn, giving it a stir. "Let's check the tables so you'll have something to do!" he said, green eyes crinkling at her, handing her a tray of drawn butter, cocktail sauce, and horseradish to take out onto the deck. He hoisted a pot of oysters and followed her out.

Her parents, well-dressed as always, descended on her as she and Tyson emerged onto the deck. "Darling! Hello!" crooned her mother, sweeping her into a hug, followed by her father.

"Hey, Cool Breeze!" he bellowed, enveloping her in his usual bear-hug.

"Hi, Daddy!"

"That little inn you got us is charming. We'll have to get it for you and Tyson for your honeymoon night. It would be just the ticket! So let's see this ring!" he laughed, watching Elaine scrutinize Stacie's left hand; she was probably thinking the diamond wasn't up to her standards in regard to size, Stacie thought, but her mother had placed her hand over her heart and was sighing, pronouncing it lovely. Good enough.

It was overwhelming at first, seeing everyone. Liz and Tom, Chelsea and Jay's parents, were there with Shelly, along with Jeanna and Rob, the book club ladies, and finally Tyson's family wandering across the deck, making her heart pound. Connie, Tyson's mother, casual in her loose linen outfit, was walking her way, a large smile on her freckled face, as if someone had sprinkled her all over with cinnamon, her reddish hair wafting about her face in the breeze. Connie was laughing and extending her arms toward Stacie, melting away any awkwardness she had previously felt. They met in a warm hug. Connie, smelling vaguely of something Oriental and spicy, patted Stacie on the back, rocking her and exclaiming her congratulations on the engagement. "Stacie, thank you for making my son so very happy!" she whispered, breathlessly into Stacie's ear, smiling at her with familiar bright green eyes, filled unexpectedly with tears. "Let me see!" she said and swept up Stacie's hand, as was fast becoming the evening ritual. Wade, Tyson's father, was behind her, as much like Tyson as she could imagine another human to look, with the exception of shorter, salt and pepper hair, and glasses. No baldness, no beer belly, nor sagging eyelids. She smiled wryly at Tyson over his father's shoulder. They hugged in greeting and he too looked at the ring, expressing his pleasure at their engagement and looking long into her eyes as she would expect of a Garrett.

Tyson stood patiently, waiting to introduce her to Jesse and Mel, and Henry. Jesse hugged her and smiled largely, a close replica of Tyson as well, only taller and heavier with waves in his hair as opposed to curls, and larger green eyes, but the same endearing dimples that appeared as he smiled at her. He presented Mel, taller than she and big-boned, with brown hair pulled into a short pony tail. Stacie liked her instantly and returned her warm hug with her own. Mel, casual in baggy shorts and leather sandals, looked at the ring as well. They conversed briefly about the engagement, remarking that they hadn't seen Tyson since their wedding two years ago. They complimented Stacie on the cool restaurant they had been hearing about, and then introduced Henry, aloof, slight and red-haired with the same powdery freckles as his mother and the same deep-set green eyes that Tyson and their father shared. She sensed he was the introverted one of the group as he shook her hand and congratulated her coolly, then took the obligatory look at the ring.

"So you're in grad school?" Stacie asked him, making conversation.

"Law school. NYU. I'm thinking about tax law."

Stacie's eyebrows rose instinctively, wondering whether his success was why the brothers hadn't seen each other in such a long time. It had to hurt.

She searched the deck for Tyson and found him at a nearby table, shucking oysters for Shelly, who had never done it before. They appeared to be deep in conversation about their investments. She smiled wistfully at him; eventually, he caught her eye and smiled back, motioning her over for oysters, and raising his beer to her. Others were gathered around the tables already, sampling the low country boil of shrimp, corn, potatoes, and sausage. She caught a glimpse of Andrew and Ava, laughing at another table and shucking oysters together. Kyle was teaching Chelsea to shuck them too, but the rest of the mountain college crew had opted for the low country boil.

Stacie noticed that Sue and Connie had struck up a conversation, no doubt about gardening or teaching. They would have so much in common, both being from New Jersey, also. Some of the men had already latched on to Wade as well, discussing boats and the upcoming deep sea fishing trip. She felt hands at her waist and realized Zack was behind her, with Nina, laughing and ready to give his rendition of their encounter with Rick at the boat dock.

"I've never seen Tyson get hot before! When Rick said that about his getting a *promotion*, he just blinked at him a minute and called him a dickhead, and then he started whaling away on his face. It was priceless! I didn't want to stop him, you know, but there were people standing around. Jerry was down there, and I recognized some people who have been coming in here for years. Rick was with that idiot Chuck who sells drugs up and down the beach. He deserved every bit of what Tyson dished out. You'd have been proud."

Tyson, who was watching Zack tell the story, motioned again for Stacie to come over. He had shucked an oyster for her and handed her a longneck brown bottle of beer. She didn't want it, but she held it to her lips to maintain the façade they had orchestrated. The oysters were delicious, and she thought about how much attention she might draw if she ate as many as she really wanted. It was difficult being deceitful, and the evening was just getting started! Tyson winked at her and shucked another oyster, offering it to her on a cracker. The shells were swept into holes in each table, from which they would fall into buckets underneath, and would then go to the town's shell recycling program, doubtlessly ending up as gravel for the commercial parking lots on the beach, or in people's gardens and walkways. Stacie and Tyson were members of the local chamber of commerce and had supported the program wholeheartedly. He was explaining the process to his father, who was familiar with it from similar practices used in Cape May. Mel commented that recycled shells were used the same way in the parking lot at the aquarium where she worked.

Henry looked basically disinterested in the conversation. Stacie watched him cast his eyes about at the girls in the group, before they settled on Vanessa, dark-haired and as beautiful as a Greek goddess. He didn't seem to mind that she appeared to be with Sam; Stacie hoped there wouldn't be trouble with these people she didn't know, who incidentally were staying in her house.

After a few moments, she wandered away from the table and caught up with Sue and Connie who were making their way back from a tour of Stacie's herb garden beside the marina. Stacie caught the end of Connie explaining Tyson's venture into cooking. "My friend Stella's husband dropped dead from a heart attack, so she was strapped without a chef for her inn, since he did all the cooking. Tyson had worked there some in the summers, so when he was home on a break from school, she asked him to help her out; that's how he found his love of cooking, so he never went back to school. I was so worried that he'd starve, being a history major. Now I worry that he doesn't ever sleep!" They laughed as they met Stacie at the door to the deck.

"Your herb garden is lovely, Stacie! I think it's wonderful that you use homegrown herbs in your restaurant."

"Well, your son wouldn't have it any other way, and Sue here is my gardening mentor. You should see her garden. It's breathtaking!"

"I guess you ladies have some wedding plans to make, so I'll leave you to it," Sue said, waving at Bets and Murph, and carrying her wine glass over to join them.

Connie wrapped her arm around Stacie. They sat down on one of the benches at the deck's edge, overlooking the sound. "This is just such a lovely place, even better than I remember! You've done such a nice job with your whole concept. And Tyson is so happy here…and with you."

"Can I ask you…are you and Wade okay with all of this? I mean, there's ten years difference in our ages, and I've been divorced. Does any of that bother you?"

Connie chuckled and her green eyes crinkled in a very familiar way. She patted Stacie's knee. "Now, I'm under the impression that you're not the type of woman who cares what anybody thinks!"

Stacie broke into a large smile of her own. "Well, normally I'm not, but this is really important to me, and I need to know…if you're both okay with it."

"Honey, my son hasn't opened his heart to anyone in so long. I never thought he would again. But right after he came here, Wade and I started to sense a real change in him, and it wasn't just that he had found Hatteras surfing! He started calling us more, and talking more. He sounded more settled and driven again. He really wanted to do well here, and then we figured out it was because of you."

"How did you know?"

"Oh, he didn't come right out and say it, but he talked about you more and more, so eventually, we just knew. And when we came here last summer and saw for ourselves, we knew he was smitten with you. May I tell you a story?"

"Sure," Stacie said, suddenly comfortable with the woman who would soon be her mother-in-law.

"I hope you won't find this embarrassing. Ty called, not long after he had gotten here. He was impressed…anyway, he was telling us that you had walked in on your husband and a girl who worked here in a rather compromising position in the office," she started. Stacie felt a vivid heat creep from her chest all the way up her throat and to her cheeks. "And after you had stormed out of the room, shocked and obviously hurt, he said you walked right back in there and said to her, 'Do you want him?' And when she nodded, meekly, I'm imagining, you said to *him*, 'Then go home and pack your clothes and don't come back. Get out of my fucking house!'" Connie said, laughter pealing from her lips.

Mortified, Stacie covered her face with her hands. "Yes, that's actually *so* embarrassing!" she whispered.

"But it worked, didn't it? The bastard never set foot in his own house again, did he?"

"No, I guess you're right. I just never expected that would be repeated."

"I had to laugh, too, when Ty told us. He thought it was the funniest damn thing he'd ever seen. He thought you were such a cute little slip of a thing, and then you went and did such a big thing as that. You won him over that day. I thought to myself, he needs a girl with spunk." She laughed again. "I guess he told you what happened to him in college," she continued on a more sober note and Stacie nodded. "He just…lost himself for a while. It was so devastating. He blamed himself for what happened to Jamie for so long. I couldn't believe my wonderful, beautiful son was just…crushed by this tragedy!" she shook her head. "But we're so pleased with your news. You are the right person for him. I know that deep in my heart. So in answer to your question, no, we don't have a problem with any of it. You need to know there will never be any secrets with us all. We Garretts wear our hearts on our sleeves. I think it's the only way to be a family."

"I agree," Stacie said, immediately knowing that she was withholding something vital. She would let Tyson tell them about the baby, if she were able to carry it at all.

"So, have you set a date?"

"We're looking at the third week in October."

Connie shrugged, "Works for us! I'm retired! I can do whatever I want! God, I love saying that! Wade will be up for anything if it finally makes Tyson happy. Count us in. We'll do whatever you want us to do."

"Will the boys and Mel be as flexible?" asked Stacie, motioning her mother over.

"I don't see why not. Henry might have mid-terms, but we can fly him back and forth if we need to."

Elaine approached and took a seat beside Stacie. Connie filled her in on the date. Stacie told them about the little chapel and the necessary permission from the bishop. Her mother suggested the two of them attend church if possible. An inner tug on Stacie's conscience was distracting her from the conversation, thinking about the baby and what she would say to Father Jack. Did it all have to be this hard? Would they be judged more harshly than she thought they deserved? They just wanted to be happy and whole again. Here she was forty years old and feeling like a misguided teenager! If worse came to worse, they could always find a justice of the peace and have their ceremony right here, where it all started anyway.

Tyson and their fathers walked up, carrying beer bottles and suggesting they sit together at one of the tables; there the conversation continued, and the date was confirmed with all of them. They discussed Tyson and Stacie's desire to keep the ceremony small with just the family and a few select friends. Then they tossed around ideas for the rehearsal dinner and planned to have the reception at The Sound Side. It all seemed amazingly simple enough that it could be carried off in just three months. Bets had already agreed to bake the cake, and Sue would be providing the flowers. Former employees and friends, Matt and Erin, would cater the event since they had transitioned into that business.

Andrew was settling himself on a stool out on the deck with his guitar, starting to play some music, as Stacie and Tyson sought out the brothers and Shelly to confirm the dates with them. Shelly, relieved that she would be out of her cast by then, was thrilled to be asked to serve as Stacie's matron of honor. Stacie had forgotten about football. Kyle was so far the only holdout since football would be in full swing; Stacie would hate for him to miss the wedding since he was the one primarily responsible for getting them together in the first place. The two of them went into her office and pulled up the UVA football schedule off the Internet; the game that day would be at Duke at noon. If he left after the game, he could be in time to join the party when it was in full swing. "If Chelsea doesn't have a performance, maybe she can come too. She doesn't want to miss this either. I'll get her a ticket to my game, and we'll leave as soon as we can get away. And don't forget, South Street will be there, right?"

"I'll do the best I can. I promise that," she said, smiling at him and ruffling his hair.

As they returned to the deck, people had started to drift over and take seats near Andrew to listen to the music. Andrew started the Happy Birthday song for Chelsea, and Stacie brought out Kyle's favorite chocolate fudge cake that had become Chelsea's favorite too. After the cake was cut and served, Stacie settled next to Shelly, who was seated alone at one of the picnic tables. Shelly was starting to get excited about the wedding and asked, "Have you thought about what colors you'll use? What are you going to wear?"

"Something loose," Stacie murmured before she had given her answer much thought; immediately, she looked sheepishly at her sister. Shelly's eyes grew large in an instant.

"No!" she whispered. "You're not...*pregnant?*"

Stacie nodded, meeting Shelly's incredulous gaze. Shelly, doubtlessly recalling their previous conversations about Stacie's medical problems, spoke discreetly. "Is this *safe?* Who else knows?"

"Just you, Tyson, and me at this moment. I hope it's safe. It's too late to be worrying about it now! I have an appointment with Karen on Monday. We said we wouldn't tell anyone until we see her. I just couldn't keep it in."

Shelly reached her hand across Stacie's lap and held her hand. "God, Stacie, you've always been so reckless! But I'm so happy for you. When do you think you're due?"

"Maybe March? I'm not sure exactly when this happened. It obviously wasn't part of the plan. We think it might have been the night of the storm," she said, looking around at all of her friends, family, and soon-to-be family. Henry was watching them, leaning against the railing with Vanessa, Sam, and Les; he raised his Bud when he caught her eye. She smiled at him.

"If it's a girl, will you name her Abigail, after the storm?" laughed Shelly.

"I don't know! That's kind of cute, actually."

Shelly held her head back and scrutinized her sister. "You know, I was thinking there was something different about you…it's your lips. They're a little fuller. You definitely have the glow, but you've had that for a while now! This is so exciting! I'm going to be an *aunt*!" she whispered, smiling delightedly. Stacie shushed her.

Tyson was suddenly at her side. He slipped his arm around her as he sat next to her at the picnic table. "Are you two sharing secrets?" he chuckled, looking at Stacie warily.

"Yes!" Shelly whispered again, eyes glowing. "And this is great news! I'm so happy for you. You'll make such a good father."

Stacie watched his pleased reaction; suddenly, he had taken on a whole new dimension in front of her eyes. She had never doubted that he wanted this—a family, a happiness he had been denied—and now she was as convinced as ever that they were meant to be together in the grand scheme of things. She slid her hand across his and he grasped it warmly, stroking her fingers, entwining his with hers. "I've heard that the Garretts don't do secrets," Stacie told Tyson tentatively.

"Well, this is not so much a secret as personal business we're trying to get on top of. I'm sure we won't be in trouble for waiting until we know what we're talking about. This is a lot of change for our families to take in at once, right?" he directed his question at Shelly, who nodded, smiling.

"But I'm sure nobody will have a problem with it!" she grinned.

Chapter 7

SECRETS

Bangelic was a hit at The Sound Side on Friday night. The soft shell crab special that ran that evening had drawn a crowd, and the regulars who came in were joined by a throng of tourists who had heard about the place. The young locals and summer people had made The Sound Side a popular hangout for after work hours as well, so the place was packed. The band's opening set was bluegrass, and everyone seemed to enjoy a change of pace from what was usually played at the coast. The bar was busy, but Ava had proven to Zack and Andrew that she was a competent member of their team. Henry seemed to be at odds without the band members to hang out with, so he sat with Jesse and Mel at the bar, conversing with the bartenders and taking sidelong glances at Lilia and Alex as they whipped in and out around him, placing drink orders and sweeping trays of beers and glasses of wine to waiting customers. Stacie had gone behind the bar to retrieve another bottle of chardonnay for her book club friends and their spouses who had secured a table near the band.

"Are you having fun?" she asked Henry, who seemed to watch her dreamily with his chin propped on his hand.

"Oh yeah," he said. "This is about as relaxed as I've been in a while," he continued, twirling his bottle around on the bar.

"I heard you learned to skim board today!" she said, smiling at him as she recalled her conversation with Kyle and Chelsea earlier in the evening.

"Yeah. I gave it my best shot. It's not as easy as it looks."

"Are you a surfer like Tyson?"

"Nah, not really. Jesse's into boats and Ty surfs. I just never got into any of that stuff. I like to fish, though. I'm looking forward to Sunday's trip."

"So is Tyson. He's really glad you came."

"Right," he said dismissively, taking a swig from his beer bottle.

Stacie walked around the bar to deliver her bottle of wine, thinking it an odd response. After serving her friends, she caught up with Tyson as he came out of the kitchen, his work finished for the evening. "Everybody's having fun," she reported. "Time for you to start."

"Yeah, I'm ready to kick back. Want to join me?" he asked. They found a table near the large one where all the parents and Shelly had gathered with their own wine and beer. Alex was at their table and took their order for a beer and an iced tea with lemon and mint.

"So what's Henry's deal?" Stacie asked Tyson after a minute.

"What do you mean?" he asked, running a hand through his dark curls.

"Hmm, he just seems to have his knickers in a wad sometimes. I get a funny feeling watching him, watching people."

Tyson chuckled. "He's probably just pissed that he hasn't snared some pretty young thing yet. Of the three of us, he's always been the moody one. Always wanting to be the best. Jesse and I could really give a shit, you know?" he said, smiling at Alex, who was setting their drinks on the table. "Henry was the one who stayed in his room most of the time…plotting to take over the world!"

"Your parents are so laid back and outgoing. It's hard to imagine any of you being like that."

"It's always been hard for him to open up. He cares way too much about what people think. So," he said, changing the subject, "do you think you flipped your sister out yesterday with the news?"

"I'm sorry I broke our truce. I just couldn't stand not telling somebody. I'm glad you're better at holding your tongue than I am! Shelly was the one I really wanted to share it with."

"Good. It's great that she's here now. You need her."

"I guess I do. I never really thought about it that way."

"I know. You're one of those women who needs to handle it all by herself…all the time."

"Oh, really?" she said, smiling broadly at his analysis of her.

His green eyes crinkled and his dimples appeared at the edges of his smile. "I like seeing you slide off into the land of vulnerability. It's really *very sexy!*" he said in a low whisper, reaching across the table for her hands. "Just think of you and me with a little baby between us in our bed. And just so you know, I won't mind getting up in the middle of the night for feedings."

"Like you'll be able to do her a lot of good!" she laughed, although the image moved her.

"Her? It's gonna be a boy. We can make the weight room into the nursery and name him *Rocky.* Anyway, I'll bring him to you and all you'll have to do is lay there and nurse him."

"No, it's going to be a girl and we're naming her *Abigail,* after the storm in which she was conceived."

"Well, she's sure to be a pistol like her mom," he said, stroking her hand. "There's so much to look forward to. We're going to have a great life…."

At that moment, Jesse and Mel appeared at the table. "Do y'all mind if we join you?" asked Jesse with a large grin on his face.

"Wow, bro, you sound like a local! Sure, join us," said Tyson, laughing at Jesse's surprising attempt at the dialect. "What happened to Henry?"

"He found some girls to pursue," said Mel. When they looked around, they found him on the deck, talking to two girls they did not know.

"So, what do you think of our beach?" Tyson asked, tipping back his bottle of Bud Light.

"It's cool…long and spread out, as opposed to Cape May, but very cool," said Jesse, rubbing his chin. Stacie noticed he had the family cleft in his chin like all the men. "See, in Cape May, we ride beater bikes everywhere. Mel and I have a car, but we seldom use it."

"You should come up and stay with us sometime, Stacie. It's a sweet place," offered Mel.

"I'd love to. Maybe in the winter, when we're closed," she thought, imagining her baby bump that would be large by then; she cut her eyes to Tyson, who squeezed her hand in response.

"And by the way, you're a very good cook," said Jesse to Tyson. "I had the shrimp and grits and it was excellent."

"And I had the soft shell crabs and collards. I didn't think I would like collards, but they're delicious!" remarked Mel.

"Tyson's are the best ever!" said Stacie; he bowed his head slightly.

"I can see why you don't come home, man," said Jesse, raising his bottle to his brother's.

"Is that still a problem?" Tyson asked earnestly, meeting Jesse's eyes. Stacie studied the interaction carefully.

"Not for *Henry*." Jesse glanced at Stacie's questioning eyes. He continued for her benefit, as Mel stroked his arm and hooked her hand inside his elbow. "See, Henry thinks of Tyson as the prodigal son, so to speak." Jesse looked at Tyson, "Does she know about Jamie?" he asked and Tyson nodded. "Henry was fifteen when all that happened, and he really never has understood the whole thing. You could say he kind of has a chip on his shoulder about it."

Tyson raised his eyebrows and appeared to take a deep breath. "That's putting it mildly. He needs to grow up."

"Yes, he does," said Jesse, as they both drained their beers. Alex was there in a flash, gesturing the question for whether they wanted two more; they nodded, and Jesse held up three fingers. "Nothing for you?" he quizzed Stacie.

"No, I'm taking a little break. It's going to be a long weekend, and I have to get up for breakfast in the morning." Tyson smiled at her and refrained from winking.

"You guys work like dogs," said Jesse.

"Not me. I don't do breakfast. That's a totally different crowd," said Tyson. Stacie fully expected him to raise his index fingers and form the sign of the cross, as if warding off something evil, such as the face of his alarm clock at 5:30 a.m.

"It's not so bad after the summer," she laughed at him. "We close from Sunday through Tuesday in the fall, and shut down around Christmas until the end of February. I'm rethinking the whole breakfast concept anyway after my crew leaves for college in another month. We're starting to do all right, so I could drop it."

"That's good for you…in this economy," said Mel.

"We've been some of the lucky ones. The music is what's saved us here. People love the music. That and the low overhead," she said, gesturing around.

At that point, the band went on a break; Stacie went to check on them and let them know how well they were doing. It was fun having young groups in that needed encouragement. With any luck, they would be back next summer if they were still together. She excused herself and went to see Jay. He and Lauren had found Tom and Liz at their table, so they were already getting stroked, and Stacie squeezed their shoulders and added her compliments to the list. To her relief, the parents all seemed to be getting along well. Sam and Les had made their way to the bar, and the other girls had wandered out onto the deck to talk to Kyle and Chelsea, where Stacie noticed Henry taking up with them, introducing them to his newfound women.

The next set was popular music, which everyone enjoyed as well. Stacie watched as the crowd became looser and the young ones more inebriated as the last set, Celtic music, began, bringing them all to a rowdy head. It was always this way, and at midnight when the lights came on, so many of them would scatter like cockroaches that the place would empty out in no time. She had been visiting with the bartenders with her elbow propped on the edge of the bar, commenting with Andrew on how versatile the band was and what a nice change it was from the usual fare.

Henry appeared beside her, listing slightly; her eyes sparkled at him, amused. "Still having fun?" she asked him, laughing from knowing what his answer would be.

"Yep," he said, mirroring her posture on the bar just two feet from her. "Are you?"

"Always," she nodded and he continued, leaning in conspiratorially.

"I know your secret," he said, low in her ear, his words sounding a bit slurred.

Her eyes widened and she froze. He looked at her with sparkling eyes that intended a strange kind of humor. "What secret is that?" she asked warily.

"He knocked you up, too. Isn't that why you're getting married?"

Stacie felt a slow boil beginning in the pit of her stomach; the heat from it began to creep up her neck onto her face. "No, it's not. I love your brother very much. And I guess you know, this is not public knowledge, so we'd like to keep it that way until we think it's the right time to make it known. I really don't have to explain any of this to you," she said, suddenly livid, understanding now how Tyson must feel about his brother. "Why are you so intent on making this ugly? Because it's not."

"He just can't seem to get it right, is all."

"Oh, just give it up! *You're not living his life,*" she said, careful her friends were not overhearing their conversation, although she realized they must see the expression on her face. She wondered where Tyson was at the moment; she hoped he would not show up right now. "That's why you're in law school, isn't it? You're just trying to show him up. That's pretty twisted. Are you just trying to prove something to your family? You don't have to do that. You should do what *you* want to do."

"Law's what I want to do. You don't know…."

"You know, if you resent him so much, maybe you shouldn't come to the wedding. I don't think I want you there." She regretted saying it as soon as it was out. How had this gotten so out of hand so quickly? Was he really as messed up as she thought? Was she over-reacting? He was drunk, obviously, but still, it was out of line. "Look, I'm sorry. I'm not trying to pick a fight with you, Henry. But don't make this bad, okay? I think Tyson would like to have a relationship with you, if you'll allow it. I don't want to get in the way of any of that. But this is up to you. Please keep this pregnancy to yourself. My parents don't even know about it yet."

"Like I said, Stacie, it's your secret. I wouldn't dream of causing problems," he said, eyes glinting at her again in an unsettling way. Bangelic was finished and the crowd was on its feet, with applause, whoops and whistles. The lights came on.

Stacie was mixing key lime pie in the mixer when Tyson came in for lunch preparation on Saturday. Sanders and Darius were finishing up the breakfast clean-up and Kyle was expected back at any moment. He had chosen to work breakfast and lunch so he could spend time with Chelsea. Stacie looked up from the mixer and smiled at Tyson; he circled his arm around her waist since no one was with them in the kitchen. "Feeling any better?"

"Yeah, I just need to remember to eat," she said, feeling less green than she had when she had gotten up that morning.

"Do you feel like telling me what's on your mind? You didn't sleep very well, in spite of that knockout sex we had last night," he said in her ear. She laughed and then sobered up quickly, figuring she had better come clean before the fishing trip tomorrow.

She turned to him, wiping her hands on a towel, and put her hand on her hip. "Henry knows."

He raised his eyebrows a notch. "Are you sure?"

"He told me. I think he overheard me telling Shelly the other night. Maybe we should go ahead and tell our parents and Jesse and Mel before they find out the wrong way."

"Absolutely," he said distractedly. "What did he say? I'm guessing it wasn't too nice."

"Well, no, it wasn't. I'm trying to like him, but I've seen his dark side. He was drunk...."

"What did he say?" Tyson repeated.

"I don't think you really want to hear it, but it was creepy enough for me to tell him I didn't think I wanted him at the wedding."

He shook his head and rolled his eyes, sweeping his fingers through his hair. "Jeez," he said.

"And then I apologized, because I don't want to stir up any bad feelings within your family...."

"If he's an asshole, you have my permission to treat him like one. He has no business coming down here and making trouble. He's my brother, but you're going to be my wife, and I won't have this shit."

"See, this is what I don't want...Why is he like this?"

"He never forgave me for coming back to Cape May and stealing his limelight. Here he was, the last one at home, getting all the attention when I show up all miserable. He didn't want me around."

"That's kind of immature, even for a teenager, don't you think?"

"I don't know. I guess we all dealt with my depression in different ways. It took me a long time to forgive myself."

"For what, Ty, *loving someone?*" she asked, flabbergasted.

He looked at her meaningfully and then chuckled.

"What?" she asked.

"That's exactly what my mother said."

"So that was why you left home again," she asked softly.

He nodded. "That, and I just couldn't handle being under my parents' scrutiny all the time. It really hurt them. It was healthier for me to move on."

"What about your job there?"

"Oh, Stella understood. We trained somebody else before I left. I'd never leave anybody in the lurch like that. That was when I took off for Florida...and then it was Tybee, and then Isle of Palms. Like I said, it was destiny that I came here and found you. Let's just be happy about it and not let Henry screw up our good thing."

"Still, he should get over it."

"We all think that. But that's up to him."

"You're way too nice."

"Isn't that why you like me?" he asked, slipping his arms around her and holding her close, as the door squeaked open and banged shut, and Kyle appeared in the kitchen.

"Hey, dude!" Tyson greeted him. "Have you decided to go fishing with us in the morning?"

"No, thanks, but I think I'll pass. It will be my last day with Chels for a while. The homeboys are hanging here, too, so I think I'll hang out with them. We can stay here and get the bonfire together so it will be ready when you get back."

"That would be awesome. We have some more oysters that we could roast out there."

"We'll take them home with us tonight…let's remember," said Stacie, feeling a renewed pang of love for this man who would soon be her husband. Then she turned to Kyle and asked, "Is Shelly coming in tonight for dinner?"

"Yeah. Chelsea's parents are bringing her. They're planning on meeting Pops and Gran here around 7:30. Mom is getting around really well, now. She's going to work over at Rob and Jeanna's company next week when Pops brings her back from moving me in at school. All she has to do is get there; then she can answer the phone and sit in front of the computer all day, or as long as she can make it."

"That's great. I know she's bored to death sitting at home."

"I know. It will be really bad when I'm gone."

"She's really gonna miss you. We all will!" said Stacie. Turning to Tyson she asked, "So who *is* going fishing?"

"My dad, your dad, both my brothers, Tom, Zack, and me."

"Andrew isn't going?"

Tyson smiled. "No. He gets seasick. He mentioned hanging out with Ava and her kids at the aquarium."

Stacie's eyebrows ratcheted up several notches. "Wow! Now that's some *destiny*!"

Chapter 8

FAMILY MATTERS

The families were told about the baby at different points during the day, and it was agreed that the news would be kept "inside" until the doctor had given them a confirmation. Mostly the news was well-received, although the Garretts were disturbed that Henry had reacted the way he had. Tyson had convinced them to let it be and see whether the situation would resolve itself. No one wanted to banish Henry from the wedding, but his behavior was disconcerting nonetheless, and Stacie felt bad about the whole thing.

The band played well and attracted a good crowd again on Saturday night, with some repeat fans in attendance. The men who were going fishing begged off early in hopes of getting some sleep before their early call on Sunday, Tyson included. Henry was not seen or heard from all day, and it was rumored he had taken up with one of the girls he had met on Friday evening. It was fine with Stacie if he chose to dodge the limelight this time; she had enough to contend with, considering a wedding and a baby on the way, and six houseguests!

On Sunday, the boys left Stacie's around ten o'clock to allow the women their shot at brunch and a relaxing day on the beach. "Tell Carole I said hello if you see her!" Stacie called to Kyle, referring to her friend, the owner of Sam and Omie's, as they piled into Jay's Jeep. Kyle took the boys down to Sam and Omie's at Whalebone Junction for their own breakfast. Lucy Murphy joined the ladies only briefly during their brunch of breakfast casserole, fruit salad, and blueberry muffins since her son and daughter-in-law and their three sons were visiting from Richmond for the weekend.

"They're packing up and heading back about two o'clock. They'll have their naps in the car. You know, they have to stick to that schedule or they turn into pumpkins!" said Murph, chopping her hand against the other several times for emphasis. "You all are welcome to use our tent, if you don't mind packing it up when you're done and sticking it in the shed. If I haven't crashed myself, by then, I'll come and join you at the beach!"

Elaine commented to Murph, "I admire you, being able to manage three little ones the way you do. After Desiree and Kyle, I don't think I have the energy to run after toddlers anymore!"

Stacie took it in silently, knowing her mother hadn't intended to slight her. And Murph didn't know the upcoming news either. Connie smiled at her, supportively, as they all sipped orange juice.

"Well, if we don't see you at the beach this afternoon," Stacie said to Murph, "you and Terry come out for the bonfire tonight. Bets and Jim are bringing Allie, and Sue and Paul will be there, along with about seven half-dead fishermen! It should be fun. We'll be cooking hotdogs and roasting some oysters around six. I *don't* think it will be a late night!"

"We might do that, and just drive home after dinner."

"Stacie," Liz spoke up, "don't you buy a thing. This is our treat tonight. You've been so gracious to host this whole shebang and give Bangelic its chance here. We're bringing the dogs, buns, chips, and right now there's a Crockpot full of Chelsea's favorite baked beans in the works! Tom has a case of beer in Shelly's fridge, and I made tea for everyone who doesn't want beer. I don't know about anyone else, but I'm going to have to dry out a while when I get home!"

Stacie smiled at her, sitting beside her sister, with Chelsea on the floor in front of her, enjoying having her hair stroked. "I'm so glad you all could come here. This has been so much fun."

"Tom was so excited to go fishing with the other men! We haven't been away like this in quite a while," remarked Liz wistfully. Stacie knew she was referring to all the time spent taking care of her mother-in-law, who had passed away earlier in the summer.

"I have something for you, Chelsea," Stacie said, walking over to a writing desk on the wall near the kitchen. She handed Chelsea a package, wrapped in cream colored paper and tied with ribbons.

"Happy Birthday! This is for you to take with you to college. Kyle's getting the same thing, even though it's not his birthday," she said, watching as Chelsea untied the ribbons and slipped her fingernail under the paper, separating it from the package. Inside was a wooden frame, covered with tiny seashells, and the picture inside it was a photo of Kyle and Chelsea on the beach in their swimsuits, wrapped in each others' arms, laughing. Chelsea looked up at Stacie and smiled.

"This is from spring break, right? When I was trying to teach him how Willie and I did the dance lifts....we weren't very good!"

"No, but it was certainly fun to watch you *try!*" Stacie said laughing, and Shelly joined in, remembering, leaning in to look at the picture.

The other women passed the picture around and Lauren commented, "This will be a good conversation starter for your new friends in college. They're all going to want to know who the *hot guy* is!"

"Yeah, and Kyle's new friends will be asking the same thing, who the hot girl is!" Emily chimed in.

"Well, I thought it would be good *girl deterrent* for him while he's away from you!" laughed Stacie.

"Thank you! I'm sure I'll appreciate it with all the Virginia girls he's bound to meet up there!" laughed Chelsea; her words made Stacie feel a small wave of sadness flow through her, remembering Tyson's story about his Virginia girl.

"Well, I'm sure no one will be able to hold a candle to you in Kyle's heart, dear," said Elaine, making Chelsea blush.

As they cleaned up the kitchen, Stacie leaned into Connie's ear at the dishwasher and asked, "Did Henry show up last night?"

"Yes," said Connie. "He was down at Nags Head with one of the girls he met at the restaurant on Friday night. She's a student at UNC-Chapel Hill. Isn't that the one with the really good basketball team?"

"Oh yeah, Carolina basketball. It's all the talk from January to March around here," Stacie replied.

"Anyway, they were at the beach most of the day and looked a bit sunburned. I'll bet he's rather fried right now!"

"Everything all right?"

"I think so, but I'm sorry you had to experience what you did with him the other night," she said, obviously disturbed. The other women were not in earshot, so she added, "There's something you need to know about Henry." She stopped wiping the counter, meeting Stacie's gaze. "He's an *alien*," she said seriously.

Stacie threw back her head and laughed her rich, throaty laugh. "Oh, God, Connie, you kill me!"

"I don't know how he emerged from my womb! He's just so different from the rest of us Garretts. I love him, like I do all my boys, but jeez, he can be such a jerk sometimes! It's *embarrassing*! I don't know what he said to you, but really!"

"Connie, don't worry about it. He was drunk."

"No. That's no excuse! He should never say half the junk that comes out of his mouth. I don't know how he's ever going to be a lawyer that way…" she said.

Stacie shook her head. "It's fine, really."

"You should have slugged him. I wouldn't have blamed you."

"You and Tyson are on the same page," Stacie laughed.

"I'm just so sorry," said Connie, pressing her hand on top of Stacie's. They went back to join the others, who had gotten into bathing suits, assembling beach bags, ready to head out to the beach. Shelly was inching down the stairs on her bottom while Liz carried her crutches for her to use on the boardwalk.

Elaine took Stacie's elbow before they headed out the door. "Darling, I've decided to stay here until your dad and Shelly come back from dropping Kyle at school. That way it'll give us a chance to visit a little more privately, and we can talk about the wedding plans. Is that okay with you?"

Stacie felt suddenly and oddly relieved, and glad. She smiled and hugged her mother. "Of course! That would be great, Mom. Do you think Daddy can handle them without you?" she asked, watching out the window her sister's progress on the crutches with her friend at her side.

"Oh, sure. They'll be fine. Shelly's doing so much better than she was even the last time we were up. She's surprised me with what a trouper she's been through all this."

"Well, do you want to stay here? You're welcome to…."

"No. I'll just stay at Shelly's. I can clean up from her guests and stay there. You and Tyson will probably like to have your house back to yourselves, anyway. This has been a lot on you, but as usual, you've done it all so well."

"I'm a party girl, Mom. I guess I like crowds."

"Well, I'm sure that will all be changing as things progress. You and

Tyson need your time," her mother said, blue eyes twinkling. "I just really miss being with you, and there's so much we need to talk about now!"

"Thanks, Mom. You know Tyson and I have a doctor appointment tomorrow. Maybe if there's time afterward, I can stop by Shelly's and tell you about it before I go to the restaurant. What if there's really no baby and we've stirred everyone up about nothing? I haven't slept, just thinking about it."

"Oh, honey, I think this is the real thing!" Elaine said, her eyes getting wide. "Even I thought it when I saw you…Wade even knew!"

Stacie's hand went to her mouth instinctively.

"Well, think about it. He's seen his wife pregnant three times. He knew what he was seeing!"

"I had no idea I was being discussed so…*thoroughly*," she gulped.

"We all think it's just lovely."

"At forty…you're not all just…horrified?"

"Not at all. It's a blessing," Elaine said, squeezing her daughter's hand. "You get changed and then let's go catch up with the ladies. Oh, and here come the boys. Perfect timing!" she laughed as they heard the boys tromping up the stairs to get their beach towels and footballs for entertaining themselves on the beach.

The fishermen arrived about 4:30 p.m., appearing fried, tired, and well-bonded, except for Henry, possibly, who apparently had been hung over from the day before and spent the trip out to the blue water in the boat's salon, sleeping it off. The trip had been prosperous since they had returned with a boatload of wahoo and tuna between all of them. There would be plenty of fish for the families to divide and take home, and plenty of stories to go along.

In the kitchen, Tyson met Stacie, fresh and clean-shaven from his shower, with damp hair and bare feet. They could hear the college girls talking and laughing while they dried their hair and got ready for the evening while the boys were showering and cutting up at the outdoor shower below them. She handed him a vodka tonic and clinked her glass of water with lime to his. "Here's to a successful trip!" she smiled. He was even darker than usual and his white baseball T-shirt set off his tan and striking green eyes in a way that made her heart swell. He took her in his arms, breathed in her perfume, and looked her over. His eyes warmed as he looked at her. He touched her shoulder. "You look really pretty in this," he said, touching her blouse, which was soft and loose and hung down over her jeans. Her hair was pulled back in anticipation of the breeze on the beach later. She looked down at her top, and spread her hands down across her abdomen.

"You'll be seeing it a lot," she said softly, meeting his bright gaze.

"You got some sun today," he smiled and stroked her cheek.

"Not nearly as much as you guys did. Was it fun?"

"Yeah, it really was. We caught a *ton* of fish. My dad and your dad got along really well, and Tom too."

"So my dad hung in there with all you young guys?" she asked, looking concerned.

"Yeah, he did great. He's what, seventy-two? You'd never have known. He was reeling that wahoo in like he was *my* age. He's as strong as an ox, your dad."

"*He* hooked it?" she asked incredulously.

"Oh, yeah! That fish was sixty pounds at least. He'll sleep like a baby tonight! Jesse and Tom caught most of the tunas. Henry had a huge wahoo on, but it broke the line as soon as we got it to the boat."

"I'll bet he was disappointed."

"Yeah, but he'll still eat good…when he's home again."

"I don't guess you two talked?"

"Nah, wasn't the time nor the place. He's the same old Henry. Never know anything's wrong," he mumbled absently.

Stacie wondered whether it was because Henry really didn't care what kind of trouble he was causing, or if he were embarrassed. Tyson changed the subject as she noticed he did whenever the topic was Henry.

"Did you ladies have a good time?"

"We did," she said, lightly; she filled him in, letting him know her mother would be staying on an extra couple of days for her sake, which pleased him. "Mom doesn't want to crowd us so she'll be staying at Shelly's. She's being *so* considerate," she whispered, bumping him playfully with her hip and encouraging him to pull her in for a kiss.

They prepared the pots of oysters and damp towels for steaming at the bonfire, and Tyson carried a table down to the beach. He rolled out a cooler of beer and soft drinks next. Stacie carried a basket with towels, paper plates, forks, shucking knives, lemons, paper towels, and water bottles for hand-washing after the oysters, and a smaller cooler with cocktail sauce and condiments for the hotdogs she and Liz had agreed upon earlier.

The Murphys arrived before anyone else, and Lucy had brought a basket filled with graham crackers, marshmallows, and chocolate bars for s'mores later. "You are *so* great! Thank you. This will be perfect!" Stacie exclaimed, hugging her friend. "We forgot the skewers," she said to Tyson.

"I'll bring them. I have another bag of ice up in the fridge, too, to bring down," he said, and he and Terry walked companionably back up the steps to the boardwalk.

She looked at Murph, wearing a yellow T-shirt proclaiming *Life is Good*, and blinked her eyes, "You did *not* iron that T-shirt, did you?"

"Well, yes, among many other things, like the socks I'll be wearing to work tomorrow and Terry's shirt. That way, when we get home tonight, we can just hang it on the closet door and be ready to hop right in it in the morning!"

Stacie shook her head in wonder. "You are truly amazing! How was the visit with the grandsons?"

"It was fun, but I'm tired! I should have taken a nap!"

"You should have left the ironing alone and slept!"

"Well, they're so cute. I didn't want to miss anything. They don't get to come that often."

Stacie could imagine how precious their time must be. Everyone always said that about their children. *You blink your eyes and they're all grown up.* Comments like that were beginning to take roost in a new place in her head.

More people were flip-flopping across the boardwalk, and bright voices and laughter were getting closer as Stacie and Murph waved at Kyle, Chelsea, and Liz. "Didn't you bring Shelly?" Stacie called, noticing Kyle carrying the crutches.

"She's making a grand entrance!" laughed Liz, brushing her dark hair away from her face in the wind. Tom emerged, carrying Shelly across the boardwalk, his nose and cheeks a bright shade of fuchsia above his silvery blonde mustache. "This was much faster. He was getting tired of waiting for her!"

They laughed, and the college crowd came next, followed by Tyson and Terry, each carrying beach chairs and towels to sit on. "Here, we can put her in the throne over here," Stacie giggled, gesturing to her beach chair, where Shelly could rest her foot out of the sand.

"Thanks! There's nothing worse than getting sand in my cast. I'm sure when they take it off a little pile of it will come trickling out!" Shelly laughed, arranging her loose linen pants around her legs as she situated herself on the chair. "Mom and Dad are right behind us," she smiled as they watched Tyson light the bonfire.

The Bangelic crew had crowded around Stacie and presented her with a spa gift card for a massage in return for her hospitality. "Thank you! This is so nice guys! It was really fun having you all stay here. Okay, who was it who ran into the wall in the middle of the night last night?" she asked, looking from face to face as they all laughed.

Sam raised his hand sheepishly, "Uh, that would be me!" he said, placing his fingers gingerly to the side of his nose. "I was going into the bathroom and ran right into the door! I thought I'd broken my nose!"

"Wasn't there a night light?" Stacie asked.

"We unplugged it to use the hairdryer," Lauren explained.

"Well, you all can come back any time. Please come back and play for us next summer if you're still together. You were a huge hit!"

Stacie made the rounds talking to everyone, and eventually, the whole crowd of friends and family had arrived. Bets, Jim, and Allie were the last to show up, and Stacie hugged her friend, who always seemed to smell of vanilla or sugar, or something delicious. "You're just in time for hotdogs!" she said to Allie, taking her hand and helping her thread a dog onto a skewer. Tyson made room for her on his driftwood seat and guided her hand, holding the skewer to just the right position near the fire.

"Not too close," he murmured. "Do you like it fat and brown or black and crunchy?" he asked, making Allie giggle.

"Black and crunchy!" she giggled again as if it were the best joke she had ever heard.

"Aahh, let's start with fat and brown and go from there!" said Bets, jiggling an oblong container with a red top. "I brought blondies for dessert!" she sang out as Jim placed a vodka citron in her hand. "Ooh, thank you! Are you my DD for the night?" she laughed; her lanky husband smiled, shook his head, and shrugged.

"Do I have a choice?" he laughed.

When Sue appeared, Stacie had to fill them in on the story of Tyson's run-in with Rick at the boat dock; the loud laughter that followed clearly embarrassed Tyson. He pretended not to notice their comments, but Bets kept him in the spotlight. When he stood to place Allie's hotdog in a bun, she took his hand, raising it high in the air as if he had won a boxing contest. "You can slay my dragons any day! Way to go, Ty!" There was applause, mostly from the book club friends and The Sound Side people who knew what she was talking about. His family looked on, bemused, and Stacie looked about, trying to change the subject. She took a towel and rattled the steamer pots with oysters while looking at him to confirm the oysters' readiness.

He took a long pair of tongs and served the oysters into small buckets. People took them to the large table to let them cool and prepared to shuck them. Stacie sat beside Shelly and began working on a few for her as Tyson joined them with longneck bottles of Corona Light, stuffed with limes; he handed one to Shelly and offered Stacie a bottle of iced tea while making a little sad face.

"It's okay," she laughed. "I'm getting used to abstaining. It's not so bad. I'm sleeping so much better."

Shelly laughed at her. "You'll be sleeping a lot now! It will seem as if you can never get enough sleep," she commented, careful to keep her voice down, aware that not everyone was in on the recent developments.

After they ate, Tyson took their shells and trash and began to clean up, getting another beer and standing around, talking with his father, Jesse, and Tom, recapping the fishing experience. Zack, Andrew, and Jay were looking at Jay's guitar; Jay offered it to Andrew to play as Ava looked on, lovely in the firelight. Conversations were settling in with people in groups of twos and threes around the fire and away from it as the heat became too much in the summer evening. Shelly and Stacie watched Kyle and Chelsea, walking hand-in-hand along the tide, away from everyone else.

"This is their last night together," Shelly commented quietly.

"How's Kyle doing with it?"

"Oh, trying to be brave, you know. He really liked the picture you gave him….They'll make it work. If they can't, nobody can."

"Oh, yeah. They'll be just fine," said Stacie, feeling a deep empathy suddenly for her sister. "How are *you* doing with it? Your son, going off to *college*? That's huge!"

"I know….I'll miss him so much. I'm hoping to go to some of his games at least. But I've been dealing with the loneliness for a while now, so I guess I'm getting used to it. This wasn't the time for me to break my ankle. At least I can drive now and get around a little better. If Kyle hadn't built me that ramp on my back steps, it would be so much harder," she said, looking at Stacie earnestly. "I'm going to be counting on you for company, you know!"

"You got it. I've been lonely too. I know what it feels like. I'm really glad you're here. I know you've dealt with so much in your life in the last few years. We'll spend lots of time together," she said, squeezing Shelly's hand. She watched as Tyson and Henry drifted off together on the far side of the fire, away from the others, where she couldn't hear their conversation, and she felt her heart skip a beat at the intense expression between the two men's faces. She knew what they were talking about and Shelly watched, too.

Tyson was speaking, running his hand across the back of his neck with one hand, the beer bottle dangling from the other. He appeared to be asking a question as Henry's hands came up defensively. Stacie saw Connie watching the interaction as well, out of the corner of her eye, in the midst of her own conversation with the other women.

Tyson was shaking his head. Stacie watched the muscle in his jaw working the way it did when he was ready to argue or when something bothered him. When he reached across and took the front of Henry's shirt in his hand, Stacie gave a small gasp, thinking they would fight, but he pulled him close and then pushed him away a little, talking to him, those piercing green eyes boring into Henry's. Henry turned his head away, but Tyson dropped his hand and twisted Henry's face back around. Shelly's hand went to her mouth as she made a sound of concern.

"I wish I knew what they were saying!" Stacie whispered.

Tyson was poking his finger into Henry's chest. Henry dropped his head, shaking it and looking back up at his brother, shaking his head again. Then Tyson's hand was on Henry's shoulder, rocking him a little; he circled his arm around his shoulders and they embraced each other, clapping each other on the back, as the three women looked on in silence, knowing none of the words but all the intentions. At that point, the brothers sat down on the sand, side-by-side, and rested their arms on their knees, talking. Tyson ran his hand through his hair, a gesture Stacie recognized as something he did when he was relaxed. Henry was shaking his head again, and it seemed that they were laughing.

Stacie felt a wave of fatigue sweep over her as she became aware that Murph, Bets, and Nina were beginning to clean up around the fire and at the table. She stood up, brushing sand off the seat of her jeans and took Shelly's trash. Everyone should be getting sleepy by now. It had been a long, action-packed weekend, and people seemed to be moving about, preparing to leave. The clean-up was now a group effort. Out of the corner of her eye, Stacie saw Henry approaching. Tyson was standing with Jesse and Mel at the same spot where he had sat with Henry moments ago. Henry took her elbow.

"Can I talk to you a minute, Stacie?" he asked. She nodded quickly, walking away from the group and the fire. He searched her eyes and let out a deep breath between his teeth. "Look, I suck at this, but I wanted to tell you how sorry I am for what I said the other night. I was *way* out of line."

"Henry…like I said, I don't want to be mad at you. I don't really know you, and I don't know what you and Tyson have been through. I just want you to be close."

He chuckled sadly. "We've never been close. We might never be, but at least he was man enough to call me on it. I should be man enough to apologize to you. You don't deserve the way I treated you. I never should have said what I did to you. I shouldn't have hurt you. I can tell you guys are not the way I thought you were."

"Did you apologize to Tyson? Does he know what you said about him?" she asked.

"Yeah," he said remorsefully and nodded. "I don't know what I was thinking. I'm sure it was really hard on him, what happened with Jamie. But, you're wrong about what I'm doing. I'm not trying to show him up. I'm in law school for me, not for my family. I hope I'm up to it. It's a lot harder than I thought, but I'm working hard. I think it's great what Tyson's doing here, and your place really suits him. It all really fell into place for him. I just didn't see it. I guess I didn't care to look."

"Well, I'm sure he's forgiven you. I have, too, okay?" she said, putting her hand on his arm; he hugged her in return. She caught Connie smiling at them from across the fire and returned the look.

"I didn't congratulate you on the baby news either. I think it's great. You're good for him, Stacie. I hope I get lucky like that someday…I mean, you know, not *get lucky*, no offense."

She threw back her head and laughed, and he finally loosened up and laughed himself. He was so awkward! They hugged each other again, and she rocked him from side to side. "I hope you'll be our guest at the wedding?"

"Yeah, I hope I can be here. Thanks, Stacie," he said, taking her hands and then dropping them as he walked over to meet Jesse and Mel and help them fold up their chairs and say goodbye to their new friends. Tyson caught her eye and winked at her from the other side of the fire.

People were laughing and shaking hands, saying goodbye to their new friends and hugging their old ones. It was sad to think everyone would be gone in the morning, and Stacie felt a little panic creep into her heart, remembering that Kyle would be gone, and she would not see him again until the wedding. He was suddenly in front of her, smiling a bittersweet smile, and she grabbed him in a bear hug.

"Wow! I can't believe I'm gone tomorrow," he said into her hair. "I'm gonna miss you so much, you and Tyson both."

She took his face in her hand and looked into his swimming pool blue eyes, so like the ones she saw each morning in the mirror. "You stay out of trouble, okay?" she said, concern crossing her face. She ran her fingers through his messy sun-streaked hair.

He laughed sharply. "I'll try my best. Hopefully, trouble won't be able to find me where I'm going!"

"And no fooling around on Chelsea," she warned him.

"Are you kidding? This is going to work with us. If it doesn't, it won't be because of me."

She smiled at his seriousness. "Well, I don't think you have to worry about her. She loves you as much as I love Tyson, if that's possible!"

"I'm glad to see you guys are back on track. I can't believe you're gonna be a mom," he said, kissing her cheek and hugging her. "Will you check on *my* mom? You know, I don't want her getting too lonely."

"Sure, we'll take care of her. Tyson has already promised her he'll do all the heavy lifting. And we're all going to try and get to a game in November if we can. *Please* don't get hurt!"

"Like I said, I'll try my best. Hopefully I'll make you proud. Say lots of prayers for me!"

Shelly was beside him on the crutches Chelsea was offering to take. "Ready?" asked Kyle. Shelly nodded as he lifted her smoothly and effortlessly in his strong arms to carry her across the beach and the boardwalk. He grunted just for humor and everyone laughed.

"My dad's had too many beers to be trusted," Chelsea explained.

"So Kyle is the designated pack mule," laughed Liz, poking Shelly's arm. They all hugged Stacie and bid her goodbye and good luck.

The Garretts were next in line for the hugs and farewells, and then everyone was gone, except for the Bangelic houseguests, who were busy helping pack up all the chairs, the table, and the coolers, and kicking sand onto the fire.

Later in the bedroom, Tyson turned down the covers as he and Stacie listened to the six young people settling themselves in for the evening. They sat on the bed and he yawned loudly.

"I feel like I'm still on the boat," he said hoarsely, shaking his head and pulling on the bridge of his nose with his fingers.

She rubbed his back with the heel of her hand. "You must be exhausted," she said.

"I don't think even *you* could keep me up tonight, as tragic as that sounds," he said, stroking her leg. Then he looked at her and cupped her face in his hand. "You and Henry talked?"

"Yes. He gave me a beautiful apology. He told you what he said?"

He nodded. "Lucky for him there were so many people around. I was about to kill him!" He looked at her again. "No one's allowed to hurt you. Just so you know." Then he kissed her slowly and tenderly.

"Do you think you guys will ever be close?" she asked, placing her hand over his, on her face, feeling sad for Henry and what he was missing.

"I don't know. That's up to him mostly. I'm willing to give it a shot if he'll meet me halfway. We're just so far away from each other."

They slid beneath the covers. He cradled her in his arms, kissing her as the household became quiet. She looked at him beside her, at his dark skin, the ring of thorns around his upper arm, the dark nipple on the firm mound of his chest, as alluring to her as a woman's breast must be to any man, she thought. She placed her hand on top of it and felt the slow rise and fall of his breathing. He slept.

In the morning, he did not stir at the sound of her alarm; she turned it off quickly, sitting up on the side of the bed, eating the necessary saltines to keep her morning sickness at bay. She showered, twisted her wet hair into a bun, and got dressed. She fixed coffee quietly in the kitchen, keeping an eye on the boys sleeping in the den on the pull-out sofa and the air mattress. After spreading cream cheese on a bagel, she slipped out of the house and made her way to breakfast at The Sound Side. She would never admit it to Tyson, but most of the time, breakfast was her favorite part of the day there. She loved the smell of bacon and eggs and toast and coffee and seeing the fresh sleepy smiles of her staff and the regular customers and tourists as she circulated through the place, refilling their coffee, watching them read their papers, listening to their plans for the day. It was busy, but oddly quiet and subdued. There was something optimistic about the beginning of each new day that put her in a good mood. A small band of older men came there every Wednesday and Friday morning, so she was sorry they would need to find themselves a new hangout. They called themselves *The Liars' Club*, and whatever stories they told each other seemed to amuse them to no end and kept them coming in…like her book club. She would miss all of that. But there would be other, new things to look forward to.

She had hardly allowed herself to imagine her life with a baby. It had been delightful enough to imagine her life with Tyson every day, which was becoming her happy reality. The support of their families had cemented the good feelings for both of them, and with the Henry situation resolved, she could relax and enjoy the next phase of her dream that was unfolding in front of her. She was still apprehensive about the visit to Dr. Walters' office today, while hoping everything was as they thought and they would get a good and hopeful report. Then, she would be able to relax, let down her guard, and begin making plans and telling people. But it was still so early, so she worried whether she could make it past ten weeks.

As Tyson drove her to the doctor's office he recapped the morning's activities at home for her. The guests had gotten up and set about cleaning their bathroom and doing laundry while he made pancakes. Emily had been nice enough to run the vacuum cleaner, and he had run the dishwasher so there would be very little to do later when she got home. She shook her head, amazed at their show of responsibility and appreciation. "I hope our kid has those kinds of manners at that age. They must raise them right in the mountains. You know, I'm not very good with *rules*...."

"We'll do our job. Our kid will turn out just fine," he said, smiling at her sideways, watching the road, and taking her hand. "Just imagine— with all the grandparents, aunts and uncles, and cousin Kyle to watch out over her, things will be just fine," he replied.

"You said *her*," she whispered.

"I don't know. After what you've said, it's starting to settle with me. A little girl would be okay. I can teach a girl to surf," he said, smiling at her with his dimples in full force. "I hope she looks like you."

Dr. Walters took them into her office after Stacie's exam and sat down at her desk, hurriedly, flipping open Stacie's file. Tyson held her hand between their chairs. Karen grinned at them, her turquoise eyes sparkling from underneath her gingery bangs. "You two didn't waste any time!" she laughed.

"We didn't plan it…Is this safe, with the tumors?" asked Stacie, her brow knit in concern.

"It's not optimal," said Karen, her kind tone unmasked by the concern in her eyes. "But these tumors are pretty small, certainly not as big as the ones you've had removed before," she said, tapping her pen on the desk. "Anyway, it looks like you're about three weeks along. You're due around the second week in March. Now, you know I'm going to be watching you extra closely, but you're going to have to adjust some things in your busy life to make sure this baby gets the best care. You don't have to do anything different in terms of your exercise. Walking on the beach is fine, swimming is okay; just don't start anything new, no training for a marathon or anything like that. Yoga is good, but start slow, and don't let yourself get overheated. I'll give you a list of nutritional requirements; the nurse will go over it with you. No alcohol for the first trimester, then maybe a glass of wine with dinner occasionally. Drink plenty of water. Don't get dehydrated. The thing for you is to cut back on your hours. You need to make sure you get enough rest and stay off your feet when you can. I know how you guys work over there; you can't keep up that pace," she said, shaking her head definitively, tapping her pen on her desk again.

Stacie nodded and Tyson squeezed her hand. They set up her next appointment, and after visiting with the nurse, she was being dropped off at Shelly's house to visit with her mother before returning to work. Tyson gave her last minute instructions before she left the cab of the truck.

"Remember, sit down and put your feet up. Don't let her put you to work. You Edmonds women don't know how to relax. I'm not letting you come back over here if you don't behave yourself," he said, pulling her face close to his, kissing her and giving her a wink before he watched her walk up the steps to Shelly's front door.

Her mother was thrilled with the good news from the doctor. She, too, insisted that Stacie sit down and rest while they talked. She handed her a glass of lemonade and they sat in the cool of the living room, chatting about the wedding plans.

"I know you and Tyson think you need to do this all by yourselves, but Daddy and I want to help. At least let us hire you a photographer. I want you to have good pictures. After all, it's going to be the happiest day of your life!" Elaine said, her large blue eyes widening further.

Stacie looked at her mother and suddenly burst into tears.

Her mother patted her hands and handed her a tissue. "Oh, honey, it's just the hormones kicking in. I cried a lot when I was pregnant too. Is that all this is?"

Stacie collected herself, accepting the tissue her mother offered, and blew her nose. "It's been such a long time since I felt this happy. And God, Mom, I'm so old! I've certainly kissed more than my share of frogs. Ty is such a miracle. You just have no idea!" she whispered the last part of it.

"And now a baby! Two miracles!" Elaine whispered back.

"Mom, pray for us…and this baby. I'm so scared after what happened the last time."

"Darling, I've been praying for you for a long time," Elaine said, patting Stacie's knee. "I have a really good feeling about all this. You girls, you and Shelly, you've really been through so much. I'm so glad you're here together and can help each other."

"That's what Tyson said too. Shelly and I are closer now than we've ever been. Kyle is doing so great, and I'm settling down. I never thought there would be any of this kind of happiness for me. I'd just sort of given up, you know? But at the same time, I didn't even know it. I feel as though I've just been living my life in a kind of limbo, going from day to day, and not really knowing why. And then Tyson came along, but I wouldn't let myself see how much he really loved me. I just can't believe it." More large tears rolled down her cheeks; she wiped them and then took a long drink of her lemonade. "When Kyle came here last summer and the three of us became so close, it's like we were all meant to find each other, you know? We all were just hiding out inside ourselves, trying to be tough and independent, not allowing ourselves to have any love in our lives, but look what happened—we're all whole people now."

Her mother squeezed her hands again. "I know, honey. You were just protecting yourself. You were trying so hard not to get hurt again. We're so glad you let Tyson in. You deserve a second chance. Love does wonderful things to us when we let it!" her mother said, smiling as Stacie wiped the last of her tears with the back of her hand, her tissue now a hot, wet ball in her hand.

"Anyway, your dad and I would like to take care of the food at the reception. We've been as excited as you are. Please let us help. You just find a photographer you like and we'll take care of it. You'll need to get on it. Those folks stay pretty booked."

"Thanks, Mom," she said and settled her head back against her chair.

"Darling, you should rest before you go back to work. You look so tired. Why don't you lie down for a while. I'll wake you when it's time to take you over."

"Okay," she murmured, letting her mother be in charge, following her back to the guest room and sliding once again into the land of vulnerability.

Chapter 9

PLANS

The first order of business with revealing her news was to schedule a meeting of the book club. Stacie called Bets, Murph, and Sue, and set it up for the following Sunday when Murph would be back at the beach. She had big plans for Terry to replace some lighting in the kitchen, so she thought she could slip away briefly, shirking her supervisory duties for a couple of hours. The assignment was to bring their favorite children's book to read to the group. The nesting instinct had already taken over, and Stacie sat, distracted in her office, going over the food order on Tuesday as Tyson joined her in the chair in front of her desk.

"Mmm-mmm!" he said to her, eyes crinkling the way she loved. He sat back, rubbing his stomach and gazing at her. "You are up to somethin'! What is it?" he asked.

She smiled and rubbed her own stomach. "I was just thinking I need to put a couch right over there," she murmured, indicating the side wall with a sweep of her hand. She knew he and Zack were going down to the duplex today for the last time to move the small couch and a few other things into storage. "Can I have yours? If I'm really going to follow doctors' orders, I'm going to need a place to rest. Not just now, but especially after the baby is born."

"That sounds *so* sexy the way you say it. Is that bad? Am I some kind of pervert or just this fiancé/father who can't get enough of his wife/mother to be?"

"Oh, it's definitely sexy, but only with you," she said, returning his smile. "I never thought being pregnant would be remotely sexy, but with you it is."

"That's because I can't love you enough….Come here," he said and went over to her purple leather desk chair, moving her up and out of it and into his lap. He breathed deep into her hair and moaned softly into her neck. "Sure, you can have the couch that was in my house. I'll bring it up here if you want it. You can crash on it tonight."

"Thank you. That would be wonderful. We have lots of plans to make. I talked to Antonio with the South Street band and they're a go for the reception."

"Awesome! Kyle will be happy about that."

"Yes, he will. And I've talked to a couple of photographers; one has the dates open if I book her within twenty-four hours."

"Do whatever you want. I'm there."

She smiled at him again and ran her fingers through the dark curls at the back of his neck. "I know you are. Isn't all this supposed to be harder than it's turning out to be?"

"Well, maybe it's meant to be, so maybe not…When are you going to tell the staff?"

"Nina already knows. She heard me retching in the bathroom before lunch. I'm guessing Zack knows then, too. I think I'll tell them tomorrow morning."

"You only have a few more weeks before the breakfast crew leaves for school. They've got it down. There's no reason you have to keep coming over here. I'll come over to unlock and make sure everybody's here. You can stay home and sleep."

She gaped at him incredulously. "You would do that for me? You, who are not a morning person, would come over and start *breakfast*?"

"Yes, ma'am. I told you I can't love you enough," he said, looking soulfully into her eyes. "It's the least I can do…and it's only for a few more weeks."

"You know if somebody doesn't show up, you'll be doing their job, running the dishwasher, cooking breakfast, hosting…."

"I've done all that stuff before. Just because I don't *like* it doesn't mean I can't *do* it. You don't need to be here. Karen said so, and I'm backing her up."

"Okay then; we have a deal." She surrendered and extended her hand for him to shake.

"Can I make a suggestion?" he asked seriously; she nodded. "Why don't you promote one of your staff members to manager?"

She looked at him, "You?"

"No, I've got my hands full. I was thinking maybe Nina. She's here all the time. She's smart. She knows the business. She'd love the opportunity. She never misses a day."

Stacie pondered this for a moment. "Actually, I've thought about this before. And she'd be my pick, for all the reasons you just said. I'll give it some more thought."

"I know. It's hard for you to give up any of your clout, but it will be fine." As he grinned, the dimples appeared in each of his cheeks so that she had to smile herself. "Don't wait too long, okay? You don't need the stress," he said, stroking the side of her face. "So, other than that, I'm gone. I'm meeting Zack at my place to clear it all out. Are your parents coming in with Shelly tonight?"

"Yes. Dad and Shelly are back from moving Kyle into the dorm. He and Mom are leaving tomorrow. I can't believe Kyle is gone."

"I know…college. That's really big. It was great having him here again this summer."

"He's like my son…" she said dreamily.

"Your son….You let him drink and have sex in your house, hmmm! I'm thinking you *do* have a problem with rules. It's a good thing Shelly has been in the dark about much of this! I've stayed out of it, but don't think I won't be all over the rules with our kid. You'd better not cross me," he warned her playfully. "We Garretts tow the line!"

"Yes, sir!" she giggled, saluting him.

The staff was thrilled with the news and the kitchen boys were not upset at all by the cancellation of breakfast after they returned to school. Stacie promised them jobs in the kitchen for next summer if they chose to return. Nina was excited about her promotion and assured Stacie that she was up to the challenge, so they agreed to begin the training immediately. She and Zack were putting away money for a nest egg so they could get married, which Stacie had expected all along, so Nina's promotion would be a big help to them.

Stacie awoke in the middle of the night, or early Sunday morning, to the feel of warm, wet sheets and a sharp ache in her abdomen. She cried out and sat up suddenly, raking back her hair and groping the sheets underneath her. Tyson's arms were around her in an instant, and he murmured groggily into her hair, "What's wrong, babe?"

"It's the baby…I'm losing the *baby*…it's *wet!*" she cried, panicked, into his shoulder as they felt around on the sheets, and then he looked, wide awake, into her eyes.

"No, no, no, it's okay. You were just dreaming!" he said, soothingly, stroking her face and holding her into his side, rocking her gently. "Are you okay?"

She sat for a moment, assessing herself. There was no pain, no blood, no loss of any child. She looked at him. "I guess so…I must have been dreaming."

"Mmmm, bad dream. Mine was much better," he said sweetly into her ear and settled her back onto the bed with him, cradling her in his arms.

"You were dreaming too? What were you dreaming about?" she whispered as he caressed the side of her face and stroked her hair away, behind her ear.

"I was holding a beach umbrella over you and our little girl on the beach. You were wearing a red dress and she was sitting in front of you on a blanket. You were braiding her hair…neither one of you knew I was there, but I was just holding this big umbrella over both of you. It got really heavy and I was sweating, but it was like I didn't have a problem holding it up…and then I heard you scream."

She ran her hand along the firmness of his jaw, feeling the cleft in his chin and kissing him there. "I like your dream better than mine. Have you dreamed about her before?"

"No," he said, "only beautiful you with your big stomach," he said, rubbing her belly and holding her quietly until they both slept again.

Stacie pulled the Cabrio into the parking lot at Wink's on Sunday, just after noon, to get last minute items for the snacks she would be serving at the book club meeting later. She was looking forward to sharing her news with her friends in just a couple of hours. Tyson had gone surfing in Buxton with Sanders for most of the day and would return about the time the ladies would be departing. She collected her purse and cloth shopping bags, but as she placed her hand on the door handle of her car, she stopped short.

Rick was exiting the store in a hurry. Normally, she would not have recognized him in his sunglasses and rumpled V-neck white T-shirt, something he would never have worn out in public, and his two day-old stubble, also highly unusual for him. But it was the familiar way he walked, and his overall appearance, the wet dark hair, brushed back, that alerted her. He seemed to be in an agitated hurry, carrying a case of beer to his black, seven series BMW. She would have expected him to have a package of diapers under his arm instead of the beer, especially at this time of day, the way she imagined Tyson would be doing about a year from now. He started the car and spun out of the lot as she allowed herself to emerge and go in to do her own shopping. She remained puzzled about his appearance while she shopped for strawberries, blueberries, and cheese and crackers. If he were going golfing with his buddies, he would have been clean-shaven, showered, and dressed for the occasion. He was always the one to be "a cut above" everyone else. It was too late to be going fishing, and she couldn't imagine he was preparing to do any kind of home improvement project. Handiness around the house was not his forte.

She thanked the clerk and carried her groceries to the car and eventually into her kitchen. The ladies arrived at two, each carrying her favorite children's book to read to the others. Murph's was *Goodnight Moon*, and Sue brought *The Runaway Bunny*. They all cried when Bets read *I'll Love You Forever*. Years ago, Shelly had given Stacie a copy of Gloria Houston's *The Year of the Perfect Christmas Tree*. It had been Liz's favorite, which she had given to Shelly when Kyle was born. It was a special story from their own beloved mountains. Stacie attempted to read it as well, but she was overcome by tears on the last page, so Murph took over for the ending.

"I've never seen you cry! What's wrong?" asked Bets, looking suspicious.

"I'm pregnant!" wailed Stacie. They all laughed and went to hug her.

"I knew it!" said Murph, in awe. "I have a box of Anna's maternity clothes in the car for you. She's hoping she'll never wear them again, after three children, but hang on to them for insurance purposes!"

"I'll bring more books too! When is this going to happen?" asked Sue, smiling.

"Mid-March we think," smiled Stacie. "There's nothing like putting the cart before the horse! We just found out for sure. Karen's going to be watching me like a hawk, and Tyson's taken me off breakfast duty. He's taking over until after Labor Day, and then it's over with altogether. He's even put a couch in my office."

"Oh, he'll make such a great daddy!" exclaimed Bets, clasping her hands with pleasure.

"He thinks it will be a girl."

"You two will make beautiful babies!" said Sue.

"It will only be one…if I can do it," breathed Stacie.

"Oh, it will be fine! You are going to be so busy!" Murph smiled at her.

"I know! I'm meeting with Father Jack tomorrow afternoon. We have to have permission from the bishop to be married, so I have to talk with him and bring in the divorce decree as proof that it's legally sound."

Sue raised her hand, remembering, "We'll have to talk flowers soon, too. I won't have much from my garden the third week of October, but we can talk about what you want and just buy whatever else we need. I'll put together some lovely arrangements and your bouquets. I did this all the time for our altar guild back in New Jersey."

"And you can have Allie's crib," offered Bets. "We're not having another one, either, so you can use it!"

Stacie laughed. "Now, Tyson and I are planning on doing *some* of this stuff ourselves, but I do appreciate your generosity. I will admit it's quite overwhelming!"

"And so exciting!" exclaimed Sue.

"Would you like to sit in the sanctuary?" asked Father Jack, brown eyes twinkling at Stacie from under his bushy dark eyebrows. He looked like a man who had spent much time in the sun; she remembered he was from coastal South Carolina and loved to fish and eat good seafood.

"That would be nice," she said, smoothing her polka dot blouse and brown skirt, and following him into the chapel, which smelled of old wood, candle wax, and flowers. The tall, arched windows allowed plenty of sunlight through the old panes and the atmosphere was serene and comforting. She twisted the sparkling ring on her finger, not as loose now, watching the rainbows it made on the wall near them.

Father Jack held up his hands in defense and said, "Don't let me talk about food today. Hearing about your menu made me so hungry the last time!"

"Oh!" she laughed. "Why don't you bring your wife and come eat with us sometime? If you like music, Friday nights would probably be best."

"Right. I do try to go to bed at a reasonable time on Saturdays. I can't *hang* like I used to," he said and winked at her, which made her laugh again. He was doing a nice job of putting her at ease. He appeared to be around fifty, but then, she was not always good at guessing people's ages. She knew he had two sons in college, and that his wife, Leigh, was a preschool teacher. Good to know for future reference, she thought happily.

"I know what you mean. Tyson and I would like to go to church, but Sunday mornings can be difficult with our schedule."

"There are other ways to participate in the parish," he offered kindly and his eyes shifted to the large envelope she held in her lap. "I see you've brought your divorce papers," he said, so she handed him the envelope.

He opened it and looked over the document with the help of his reading glasses before setting it aside.

"So, it's been over two years that your divorce was finalized," he said and she nodded. He pondered a moment. "Can you tell me what attracted you to your ex-husband in the first place?"

"Do you mean other than stupidity?" she grinned openly. He laughed good-naturedly, but looked at her earnestly, so she continued, "I was definitely old enough to know better, but I was tired of being alone. He wasn't married like some of the men I seemed to attract, to my dismay. He was handsome and charismatic and had money. He made me feel special at first, I imagine, in that trophy-wife kind of way."

"So what went wrong?"

"We…just weren't on the same page. I had more settled values and I wanted a family. He didn't, I discovered, when I learned I was pregnant into the second year of our marriage," she said, looking down. "I ended up having a miscarriage, and from there, it spiraled downward and I sort of lost my sense of self. When he had an affair with one of our employees, that ended it, essentially. Now he's married to her and they have a child."

Father Jack was quiet a moment, taking it all in and watching her. Finally he asked, "Have you forgiven him?"

"No," she said quickly and too loudly for the situation; she was suddenly embarrassed and could feel her face flame. "I've never considered it, frankly. Why…why would I?" she asked him honestly.

"Less baggage between you and God…and between you and Tyson," he said, and she nodded, beginning to understand. Maybe if she had forgiven Rick, then the whole situation with Kate would not have set her off the way it had. Maybe Tyson would not have felt the need to avenge her and slug it out with Rick at the boat dock that day. Maybe she would stop dreaming about losing her baby most nights….

"Are you saying I should *talk* to him again?" she asked tentatively.

Father Jack shrugged and smiled at her in an amused way. "That's your call. But you don't have to. It's for you, really. I guess what I want to know is, do you feel as if you've healed from your distress over all of this? Have you moved on? You need to know for Tyson's sake and yours...."

She thought a moment. "I thought I had. This is a whole new dimension I haven't considered."

"What is it about Tyson that drew you to him? How did you meet?"

She told him the story of The Sound Side, and how it had eventually become hers. She and Rick had hired Tyson shortly before she had evicted Rick from the house. She told him about the affair and how Tyson had basically run the place while she floundered around trying to regain her bearings. She told him about the summer Kyle had come and how the three of them had bonded, and eventually, how she had fallen in love with Tyson when Kyle left for school.

Father Jack listened to her with rapt attention. When she finished he asked, "What would you do if the bishop were to deny permission? Not saying it would happen, but just what if?"

"We'd go to Town Hall and find a justice of the peace," she said without hesitation. "I know God has brought us together after all we've been through. Tyson Garrett would walk through fire for me, and I would do the same for him," she said with conviction. "He is my miracle, after all these years, and I won't live another day without him." She took a deep breath and swallowed as he nodded and met her eyes with his own brown ones. "I have another miracle, too. We're expecting a baby."

Chapter 10

THE CHANGING OF THE GUARD

Over the next two weeks, the restaurant staff dwindled as her college employees left the beach to head home and then on to school. Stacie and Nina sat at the bar chatting with Ava on her last day of work before leaving with her "family" and returning to Charlotte to teach at one of the local high schools. Nina flipped through the pile of applications in front of her, showing Stacie one for a dishwasher and one for a server, both of whom she had called back for interviews, and both of whom would be arriving soon to speak with them.

"Are you ready to make your first hires?" Stacie asked Nina, eyes sparkling, as Ava slid two glasses of iced tea with lemon and mint their way.

"I think so. You'll find this interesting. Both of these applicants put down Pompano's as their last place of employment," Nina said, raking her curly blonde hair over to one side. Her statement hung in the air like a question.

Ava's eyebrows rose and her greenish-brown eyes met Stacie's. "I heard from a friend who still works there that some people haven't been getting paid. I wonder if that's why these guys are coming over," she said as Zack emerged from the kitchen, easily carrying a large rack of glasses, steaming, from the dishwasher.

He had obviously overheard the conversation and nodded, knowingly. "That's what happens when you put your profits up your nose," he said matter-of-factly.

Stacie looked back and forth from one face to another. "You think Rick is using coke again?"

"I don't think he ever stopped."

"Even after the baby was born?" Stacie asked, feeling troubled for the child's sake.

Zack shrugged. "Could be."

At that moment, a short wiry man with sallow skin and thinning damp blonde hair with matching mustache swung through the front door, adjusting the rolled up sleeves of his plaid shirt. He looked vaguely familiar, and then Stacie recognized him from years ago when he worked at The Galleon, Rick's first restaurant. He saw her and smiled immediately.

"Hey, Billy!" she said, walking over to greet him and shake his hand.

"Hey, girl; it's been forever," he said, hugging her briefly. "Wow! You haven't changed a bit. This place is great!" he said appreciatively, hitching up his jeans and having a look around. "I can't believe I've never been in here. I've always heard the bands are good and the food is even better. Are you hiring?"

"We are indeed. I'd like you to meet our manager, Nina Douglas," Stacie said, gesturing to Nina and indicating that they sit at a table near the bar. Billy waved at Ava and followed Nina to the table where they could speak privately. "So, what's going on over at Pompano's? Is there some kind of mutiny?" she asked, a hint of amusement to her voice, but Billy did not smile.

He ran a hand across the bristles of his mustache and cast his eyes around as he made himself comfortable in the chair. "I don't like to say. You know, I've stuck with Rick for a long time, but enough's enough. I haven't gotten regular paychecks in a month now, and I've got mouths to feed and bills to pay," he said, tapping his fingers on the table and looking like he could use a cigarette. "I've been hearing how solid you are, and I can use some of that right now," he said frankly. "I'll work whatever hours you've got, but I need at least thirty."

Stacie looked at Nina. "No problem," Nina said. "Would you like to have a look around the kitchen?" He nodded vigorously, so they rose to take a tour. Stacie gave her the nod, knowing Nina would have him fill out the appropriate tax forms and add him to the schedule.

The next person through the door was Chrystal, another long-time former Galleon employee who also greeted Stacie with a hug and a bittersweet smile. After they had exchanged pleasantries and Ava had served her a glass of water, she sat with Stacie at the next table and filled her in, twisting her long dark ponytail, chomping on gum, sighing, and rolling her brown eyes, heavy with makeup. "I don't know what Rick is doing, Stacie, but it's just a matter of time before the bottom falls out. I need a job, so I figured now's a good time to check it out when kids are going back to school. I've always made good money at Pompano's, but I think it would be stupid for me to stay there." When she saw Billy return into the room, she shook her head. "This will really piss Rick off with everybody jumping ship and coming over here."

"Did a girl named Kate ever work over there?" Stacie couldn't help asking.

"Yeah, she was a server until about a week ago. She went back to school too. She worked here, didn't she?"

"Yes, so I'd say I'm only about one up on Rick at the moment," Stacie smiled reassuringly. "And that's the way I like it!" she laughed, and Chrystal joined her in the sentiment.

"She flirted her butt off with him, but oddly enough, he didn't pay any attention to her. I heard she was fired. Think she was getting back at you?"

"Could have been," Stacie said absently. Then she became serious again and looked at Chrystal. "Is Rick doing a lot of coke?" she asked quietly.

Chrystal averted her eyes. "I'd say probably more than ever. It used to be that he was more discreet. Now it's like he doesn't care."

"What about Torie and their daughter? Has he still not gotten a *clue?*"

Chrystal sighed and shook her head. "I don't know, Stacie. I don't see how she puts up with him. I love the guy, don't get me wrong, but he's ruining his livelihood."

Chrystal smiled at Billy where he sat down at another table to fill out his forms. Nina now joined them to talk with Chrystal about hours and availability. As Stacie got up to retrieve more tax forms, she greeted Andrew, who was just coming in the door. His longish brown hair was brushed back far enough that Stacie caught his poignant glance at Ava and the sigh that followed. It would be their last evening together.

She closed her eyes to the fluorescent lighting of the hospital room, remembering the pastel plaid curtain that, just moments ago in the ER, had shielded her from the woman on the gurney beside her, who was vomiting into a pink basin. None of this was pleasant, and the quicker she could banish it all from her memory, the better. Karen Walters had rescued her, and the nurse had brought them into this cold room, with the bright fluorescent lighting, handing her the little short-sleeved gown to change into, but at least the room was private.

Stacie opened one eye and looked at the table beside her where the nurse was assembling the arsenal of graduated steel rods with bullet-shaped ends, designed for the gradual expansion of her cervix to allow the leftovers of her pregnancy to be removed. She turned her head away abruptly. He sighed again and paced the small room, making her want to close her eyes again. The intravenous drug was taking effect; she began to feel slightly weightless and dead from the ribs down. Just get it over with, she thought as a tear slid down the side of her face. He did not notice, and Karen's grim expression registered her disapproval of him with each move he made in the small room. He did not even hold her hand. She felt Karen's warm fingers touching her face, wiping away her silent tears as she opened her eyes to see Karen's turquoise ones gazing compassionately into hers.

Sunday morning was heavy and overcast. When she emerged from the bedroom to the rich aroma of Tyson's favorite bold coffee, she realized he had been listening to the latest storm forecast on TV and checking his stocks on his laptop. She curled herself up, snuggling beside him on the sofa, and he offered her a sip of the coffee. She took the cup and sipped slowly. "Good morning. I'll get you a cup. Want some?" he asked, kissing her lightly on the forehead. She shook her head. Coffee was not something she could stomach these days; she would opt for tomato juice and toast later. She stroked the pink plaid fabric of the pajama pants she seldom wore when they slept together. After the dream at dawn, she had put them on thinking they somehow could make her comfortable. The dream had left her unsettled and irritated that Rick was still imposing on her life. Tyson closed the computer and slid it under the sofa, stretching his arm around her shoulders.

"Is the storm coming this way?" she asked to divert attention from her mood. She took one more sip of the coffee and then handed back his cup.

"Nope. It's making landfall in Wilmington, but we should get plenty of wind and rain out of it. Suits me. I have nice memories of holing up in here with you," he said, stroking her hair and holding her closer. She smiled and wrapped her arm around his torso, soft in the old white T-shirt he wore. "So what did you dream about last night?" She knew he would be curious after waking to find her already awake. He had taken her into his arms just as the first hint of light came in the windows. Touching him softly in the darkness, feeling him awaken and make love to her, usually soothed her back to sleep, but it hadn't this time.

"I was reliving the miscarriage all over again…and being in the hospital for the D and C." He was quiet, waiting for her to tell him more. She shook her head slightly. "I just don't understand why I keep dreaming about this stuff."

He pulled her a little closer and rubbed his hand up and down her arm slowly. "You're scared. I get that, believe me. I think it's the way we prepare ourselves for the worst. But it's going to be fine," he said softly and kissed her on the top of her head.

"How are you always so sure?" she asked, looking into his lap.

She felt him shrug. "Second time's a charm? I just think…you need to have a little faith. If you can make yourself see something, you can believe it. I think we make our own breaks."

"Is that what you do?" she asked, stroking his arm with her thumb, feeling his breathing and resting her face on his warm chest, feeling him nod. "Do you believe that things are meant to be?" she asked, looking up at him tentatively.

"I think if you want something bad enough, then it's meant to be. It's how I found you. It's how I knew you'd be mine someday. I set my sights on you a long time ago, maybe even before I ever saw you…and look at where we are now. It'll be fine," he murmured.

"Do you think God has a plan in all this?"

"Oh, God and I go way back, making plans about you," he said, causing her to smile into his shirt. "I talk, He listens; He talks, I listen. Don't you wonder how you ever got pregnant in the first place?"

"So you prayed about me?"

"All the time, baby."

Later, they lay leisurely in their beach chairs, the sand still wet from the outgoing tide, and listened to the summer noises, the cicadas in the dunes, feeling the heavy humid air that hung breezeless around them. It was still early, but hot already; only a few people were about, walking on the beach. The sky was the dull gray of late summer and the waves, what little there were of them, took their time lapping onto the shore and washing back out, almost noiselessly…the doldrums. The birds seemed lazy as well, and the neighborhood osprey circled languidly above them. Thankfully, it was not a day for surfing, and Stacie was glad to have Tyson to herself. He had stayed with her more and more lately as she had taken more time away from The Sound Side to rest and take care of herself. It seemed she could never get enough sleep, and she often found herself pleasantly drowsing here on the beach.

She made herself try his exercise in faith, thinking of hopeful dreams, visions of birthday parties. This time she imagined a little boy, with dark curls, eyes as green as grapes, and heart-stopping dimples, blowing a roll-out noisemaker, and blowing out four blue candles on his cake. She imagined him older, and suntanned, with Tyson on the beach, untangling the string of a kite, and then casting a fishing line into the surf under his father's guidance. She imagined herself cleaning up his skinned knee as he sat on the kitchen counter, rubbing tears fiercely from his eyes. As so often happened when she had these images, she became so overwhelmed with love that she had to reach out for him and touch his arm. He responded the same way, and soon he was sitting beside her on the edge of her chair, stroking her hair and kissing the palm of her hand.

They strolled aimlessly on the beach and headed back to the house for the outdoor shower. Later they would stop by the produce market, getting what they needed for the week. Stacie would visit with Shelly, and Tyson would do her heavy chores. Then they would all go to dinner at another favorite restaurant on the beach and get caught up on what was happening with Kyle at college, with football practice, and how Shelly's new job was going.

Stacie and Shelly sat side-by-side on the yellow flowered couch in Shelly's sunny living room and poured over the bridal websites. It was so much better than shopping, which was sure to be an ordeal with Shelly's cast, unless they used the wheelchair Liz had loaned her. Shelly couldn't quite bring herself to live that image in a mall somewhere.

"Ooh, I like this one!" Shelly crooned over a mid-calf length silky ivory dress with a long and elegant halter tie, a deep cut back, and a loose fitted flowing skirt. "When are you ever going to start showing?" she muttered, cutting her eyes at Stacie.

"Mmm, I've seen that one before. I love that one too. It's beautiful," Stacie agreed, thinking it was just the right style for the casual wedding she had planned. She had promised Tyson he would not have to wear a tux, but it saddened her that she wouldn't see him dressed formally. She was sure he would be stunning. But it really wasn't them. He was determined to wear his nice dark suit that he looked fabulous in, and she could dress it up with the right necktie. She had only seen him dressed up once, a couple of years ago when they were at Erin and Matt's wedding, the cooks who had worked at The Sound Side and left to start their own catering business. The two of them would be catering their wedding this time. But oh, how hot Tyson Garrett had looked that day!

Stacie scrolled the laptop's mouse on the coffee table to click on her next idea. "I think we should get you this green dress that would go with it so nicely…and Tyson can wear a matching green tie that will make his eyes pop!"

"That's the best one…this green will go nicely with the flowers too," Shelly commented, stroking her neck absently. "It's the same color as the hydrangeas." Stacie thought about her plans with Sue for the flowers, the green hydrangeas with red and orange roses and pale yellow snapdragons, and a bouquet of creamy roses for herself with green hydrangeas.

"Okay, checking your size, and…it's *available*! And," after two more clicks, "*so is mine! Add…to…shopping cart.* Done!" Stacie cried joyfully and they laughed. "One wedding, planned! Piece of cake! Now all we have to do is meet with Father Jack a couple of times, get the word from the bishop, and we're good to go. I'm not doing another damn thing!"

"Wow!" Shelly said admiringly. "That would never be me. I don't see how you can be so relaxed about it."

"Well, don't forget, I'm having a baby too! I have to put all of this into perspective."

"I'd have five million things on a list. It wouldn't even be fun. It *wasn't* very much fun as I remember…except the wedding day, when it all came together. Then I guess it was all worth it," Shelly said wistfully.

"It definitely was," Stacie said, squeezing her sister's hand as they remembered. "You had the fairy-tale wedding with the poufy white dress and everything."

"So much for *happily ever after*, right?" said Shelly ruefully. "You guys are doing it right. You're putting it all in the right perspective. You've put your happiness before anything else. And you love each other so much. I'm really happy for you, Stacie. Maybe I'll have another shot at what you have someday."

Stacie smiled compassionately. "If you want it, I know you will. You deserve it. I'd love to see some fantastic guy sweep you off your feet."

"Well…I'm not there yet, but maybe someday. I *like* being single and unattached. I'm really enjoying doing this with you right now, though. If I ever do it again, I'm putting you in charge of my wedding!"

Stacie refused to have a bridal shower. If she and Tyson didn't already have two of everything, they were cleaning out other stuff they didn't need. She had no reason for sexy lingerie, already being pregnant, and it only stayed on for about five seconds anyway, so it was a total waste of her friends' money. They didn't have a yard, so there was no need for gardening tools. And their kitchen arsenal was out of this world. She was all about a party, but told them all no presents, please. Everyone was exasperated with her for being so difficult, but seeing as how everyone liked the party idea, Bets and Jim had the four couples over to their house for *boeuf bourguignon*, and a decadent chocolate cake with raspberry sauce for dessert. Stacie's friends were exceptionally merry with all the merlot they drank, and Stacie sat back, marveling at how they transformed into comedians with such a nominal amount of alcohol. She attempted to drink a sip or two, but as with the coffee, she had lost her taste for wine.

When the Murphys and the Colemans left, Bets and Jim checked on Allie, who was finally off to sleep, and returned to the kitchen with impish grins.

"I hope you don't mind, but Jim and I got you something!" Bets giggled, nudging her husband.

Tyson and Stacie exchanged curious glances. "Sex toys?" Tyson asked warily. Bets howled with delight.

"No, but I wish we'd thought of it…actually we did, but y'all are way past those!"

"Actually, it was something you mentioned to Tyson, Stacie," said Jim with a twinkle in his eye. Stacie shot Tyson a suspicious glance.

"Are you in on this?" she asked him, her curiosity growing.

Jim laughed at Tyson's guilty face and said, "We have to hand it to Allie. She didn't let the cat out of the bag, so to speak." He looked from face to face and then Bets threw up her hands.

"Okay. Go sit down on the couch and I'll get it!" she laughed excitedly, going down the hall to the bathroom in their master suite.

Tyson took Stacie's hand and led her to the couch, where she sat beside him apprehensively, more confused than ever. Bets returned in a moment, holding a sleepy looking brown and tan Siamese cat in her arms. Stacie gasped.

"This is Mojo," Jim introduced the cat. "And he's yours if you want him."

Stacie's hand went to her mouth as she exclaimed, "Oh, he's gorgeous! How did you get him?" She looked at Tyson, who appeared to be not the least bit surprised. "You were behind this?"

A slow guilty smile crept across his face as he shrugged. "I figured we needed the practice, taking care of something *alive* before the baby comes. And I know how weird you feel with all this new time on your hands. Now you can have some company while you're resting and I'm not around."

"This guy's been my patient for years now. He was the pet of a lady who came in for several years," Jim explained. "She went into the hospital a couple of months ago and died last week. They were great friends, so he's been in mourning for her since she left him with us at the office. We'd keep him ourselves, but Bailey is not very welcoming," Jim said, referring to their Jack Russell terrier, which explained why he was banished to the backyard tonight.

"Oh, he's just *beautiful.* And how sad for them!" Stacie said, standing and reaching for the cat, who allowed himself to be transferred carefully from Bets' arms to her own. She gasped again, "Look at these blue eyes! *Mojo!*" she whispered and stroked his soft fur.

"I think she's in love!" Jim remarked to Tyson.

"Yeah, I've seen that look before," Tyson said, reaching to stroke Mojo's fur.

"Get used to it, man. First it was Bailey; then it was Allie. Pretty soon, you're just gathering dust in the attic!"

"Nonsense!" Stacie said, winking at Tyson. "You'll never be replaced."

"Oh, don't go getting mushy!" complained Bets.

Mojo pressed his head up under Stacie's chin and began to purr. "Sold!" she murmured with a smile.

"Well, in that case, we also got you some cat food, a litter box, and some litter," said Bets, going to the back porch and producing a box of cat-care equipment for them to take home.

"He's declawed, so you can't let him out to prowl around the neighborhood," Jim explained. "His shots are up to date and he's in great health. Just a word to the wise, when the baby comes, don't ever let Mojo sleep in the same room. Keep the door shut and keep him away from the crib. Sweet little kitties like this have been known to suffocate babies," Jim said, raising his eyebrows for effect.

Stacie and Tyson nodded somberly. "How old is he?" Stacie asked.

"About five years old. He's a great pet. I've never met a Siamese that was as gentle. It might take him a couple of days to get acclimated, but he'll be your buddy."

"Thanks, guys! I never would have thought to ask for a pet, but he's awesome!" Stacie said, stroking the back of his head as he slid his chin up her shoulder and purred even louder.

In the morning, Stacie padded into the kitchen and found Mojo doing figure-eights in and out of Tyson's ankles as he stood at the stove, pouring pancake batter onto a griddle. The smell of eggs had begun to turn her stomach, but he must have remembered her saying that blueberry pancakes were her latest craving. She ran her hand through her tangle of blonde hair and tied her robe, snuggling beside him, kissing his shoulder. "Hey," he said, his voice still a bit thick with sleep.

"Good morning! You boys look awfully chummy this morning. I'm surprised Mojo is still speaking to you after you *hurled* him off the bed in the middle of the night," she said, picking up her cat and cradling him in her arms, stroking his head.

He shrugged. "Well, it's one thing to snob us off all night, but then to think he can hop up there with us and get a piece of my action, nuh-uh!" he said, shaking his head. "I'm not having *ménage à trois* with any *cat!*" he said indignantly, dropping blueberries onto the soft disks on the griddle.

"Well, I'd say he's forgiven you."

"Nah. He's just hungry."

Stacie laughed, setting Mojo back on the floor. She poured herself a glass of milk and went to get his bowl, filling it with dry cat food and setting it beside the pantry door. When she rubbed his soft head, he instantly began to purr loudly. Mojo gazed at her with large soulful blue eyes before he curled his tail around himself and dug in. "I hope there's not going to be any jealousy around here," she said with mock seriousness.

"Yeah, it's like Jim said; pretty soon I'll just be gathering dust in the attic," he muttered, flipping her pancakes and readying a plate. Then he smiled at her and she laughed, sliding her arms around his waist.

"Don't worry. It'll never be like that with us," she murmured into his back. "It's like Father Jack said, 'The children are the visitors, but you have each other forever.'"

He nodded. "Hmmm…the children and the cats. I like that part about forever. I can do forever with you."

"Good, 'cause you're pretty much *stuck!*" she reminded him with a smile.

Chapter 11

BUSINESS IS BUSINESS

Between the doctor visits, the sessions with the priest, some wedding arrangements, and training her new manager, Stacie's schedule had not changed much since breakfast was axed from the day at The Sound Side. Shelly had been the one to point out to her how exhausted she would be if she tried to balance all of that on top of the morning meal. Nina was learning fast and was adept at taking over the new responsibilities. Some vague animosity was in the air between her and Zack, but Stacie assumed it was because the job of manager had been offered to Nina and not to him. Stacie had never considered that her move might cause a rift between her two best employees, and that they cohabitated did not help the situation. She sat in the office, dim and cozy with lamp light, crowded now with the small couch from Tyson's former house, pondering how to remedy this situation. She twirled a strand of her blonde hair around her finger as Zack peeked in to see her.

"Hey, you busy?" she asked as his huge shoulders loomed in her doorway, accenting his black T-shirt that broadcast her establishment.

"No. I just came to tell you we're out of the new pinot noir you like. They didn't send it again."

"Crap. That's the second time. I'll call them."

"I already called them. Is that okay?"

"Of course. Sit down a minute. I've been wanting to talk to you about some management ideas I have." He eyed the couch, but took the chair directly across from her in front of her desk. He began flicking his thumbnail against his index finger as he waited for her to collect her thoughts. "You know, as I get farther along, and then when I go out with the baby, I'm going be relying on you more and more to take care of the bar. I mean, you already do, but I want you to manage it officially, do all the ordering, take care of the musicians, the hiring, the training, closing up, and continuing to make the deposits…all that stuff. Nina's got the rest of it under control, and Tyson's got the kitchen in great shape, but I want you to be the bar manager. Andrew can help you with the music if you want, but this should be your deal. It'll be worth your while if you'll do it."

He nodded and pressed his lips together as if it met with his approval.

"So you'll do it?"

"Sure," he said, nodding again and looking satisfied. "We can use the money. I won't let you down."

"I know," she smiled at him. "You've been great all these years, and I appreciate you sticking with me all this time. I couldn't have made this place what it is without you."

"You deserve a break, Stacie," he said kindly. "Just let me know what you need me to do." She smiled at him, hoping that was all it was between Nina and him. She would find out soon enough, she supposed.

To replace the college help, Stacie and Nina had hired Angie, another hostess, and Bobby, a cook to help Tyson, both of whom had jumped ship from Pompano's. The bands and other musicians were regulars now and had queued up to get spots once or twice a year, so it was nice to know what she was getting. Andrew played on weekends once a month now that summer was over, and Zack could handle the bar by himself those nights. Stacie usually pitched in when he needed her, but after October, the crowds would be thinner and she could take a step back. She had planned to work only a small number of hours after the wedding anyway, and they would be closed altogether from Christmas through the end of February.

The wedding plans were coming along nicely. The bishop had finally granted them permission to marry, even with the baby on the way. Recognizing Tyson and Stacie's commitment to each other, paired with their age and maturity, Father Jack must have put in some kind and convincing words on their behalf. Shelly was planning to purchase a rental beach house as a secret investment for Kyle, and she offered to house the entire Edmonds-Garrett party there for the wedding weekend. Tyson had offered to help with the plans, but so far, Stacie had only required his opinion on things and had not sent him on any missions or given him jobs to do. They had gone to Bets' house together on one occasion to taste different cakes, which had been enjoyable, but she had handled the rest of the plans in typical Edmonds style, all by herself. They had agreed wholeheartedly on one thing when they discussed the invitations—no presents. It was easy to arrange so much online and through emails and phone calls, which pleased Tyson, who would literally lead her to the couch and lift her feet to the coffee table, setting the laptop in her lap, the phone beside her, bringing her lemonade or iced tea. Mojo became her assistant and curled into a ball next to her, dozing most of the time, and sometimes, she did the same thing. It was generally pleasant business.

Father Jack had taken her up on her offer, so one Friday night in late September, he brought his wife, Leigh, to The Sound Side for a late dinner and stayed after to hear Andrew play. When they arrived, Stacie was surprised but pleased to see them and hurried back into the kitchen to let Tyson know they were there. He came out to greet them when they were served their seared scallops, and when they left, Father Jack was extremely complimentary and promised to return soon.

Tyson and Stacie made an effort to go to church too, rewarding them-selves with Sunday afternoon naps, snuggled on top of the bed with Mojo at their backs, like three spoons in a drawer, dead to the world. It felt right and sweet to have Tyson standing beside her, sharing a hymnbook and listening to him sing the hymns she remembered from growing up in the church as he had. She liked seeing Tyson dressed up for church. They looked at themselves in the mirror and remarked that they looked like respectable parents, ready for the PTA, the dance recital, the baseball banquet, or chaperoning the prom. No, they were sure their child would never stand for that! She got better at dreaming the good dreams, and the old haunting ones began to fade week after week. Rarely a cross word passed between them, and the business, the wedding, and the baby were all moving along nicely.

One Thursday afternoon after a rendezvous at the florist with Sue, Sta-cie drove toward the restaurant on the beach road, a different route than she normally took, which was pleasant, and not as busy as it would have been just a month ago with the tourists, gone now, back to school and back to work. She had put up the top of the Cabrio in case the forecasters were right about the latest storm due in this evening. As she passed the produce market she and Tyson loved, she craned her neck to see what was there: tomatoes and Vidalia onions. She should get more before they were gone. Pompano's came into view next, so she looked inquisitively into the parking lot for Rick's black BMW; it was there with two other cars. She checked the door to see whether a sign indicated anything other than "OPEN," but the open sign was there. She drove past, pondering Father Jack's question to her back in early August. *Have you forgiven him?* She had been caught off guard by the question, and she had thought about it numerous times since that meeting, wondering what it could mean, and what she had to gain by acting upon it.

On an impulse, she pulled the Cabrio into the bank parking lot and turned left, back onto the beach road and drove by the restaurant again, chickening out at the last minute and passing it again. She pulled into the lot at the produce market and got out of the car, standing up too quickly, feeling the little warning tug in the lower section of her stomach that happened often, reminding her that she was a mother to be who needed to slow down and take her time. She shook her head as if trying to clear cobwebs and wondered what she was doing. She used the time to purchase beautiful red tomatoes and Vidalia onions, and some flowers to put on the table for Tyson's birthday tomorrow. Thirty-one. She remembered being thirty-one, she thought ruefully. She had been married to Rick Boutwell, and at the time, she had thought she was the queen of the island. She was working as a liquor distributor and traveling some. She came home each Thursday or Friday and the party would begin until the end of the weekend when she would head out to another place on Monday morning. For Rick, maybe the party never stopped. She soon realized that all the celebrating they did was not special. Every day for Rick was a celebration of some sort, but she could not keep up. She found herself sighing as she paid the cashier and carried her bag back to her car. She sat for a moment, caught off-guard by her close proximity to the restaurant, feeling curious and anxious. Her palms began to sweat as she took the steering wheel and drove back onto the beach road.

As she approached Pompano's for the third time, she slowed and pulled into the paved parking lot, slowly parking her car in the space beside the BMW. She took a deep breath and got out. Was she ready for this?

What was she doing here? She ran a hand through her hair, got out of the car and walked up the clean, wooden steps, looking up at the neon blue and yellow fish sign over the door. She pulled open the heavy door, whose handle was a large shellacked boat oar. Inside, it was dimly lit and cool. A large saltwater aquarium was in front of her with stunning and colorful sea life swimming around before her eyes. A server in a black dress shirt and a neatly trimmed beard appeared to ask whether he could help her.

"Is Rick here?" she asked, hesitantly.

"Sure. Would you like to sit in the bar? It might be just a minute. Can I tell him who's calling?"

"It's Stacie."

He nodded and ushered her into the bar and seated her at a table. "Would you like something to drink?"

"No, thanks," she smiled at him, and he was gone. She was the only one in the place. It was 3:30. No one was ever in a place at 3:30. Soft jazz played in the background, and she tapped her fingers nervously on the table. What the hell was she doing here? She regretted giving her name. She could just get up and leave. No blood, no foul. It could be ugly, she thought just then. With all the employees who had come over to her side, it could be a really big stink, actually. This was not what she had in mind. Was she being nosey or noble? She wasn't sure. She sighed, checked her watch, and listened absently to the music. Dave Koz, she thought, recognizing the sax and the tune she had heard before. She stood impulsively to scoot discreetly out the door; he would never know what happened.

"Stacie?" his voice was behind her, sharp and not exactly friendly. She was not surprised and turned to look at him, setting her yellow purse back on the table. This confrontation was going to go down, whether she was ready or not.

She mustered her most confident voice. "Hey, Rick," she said, raising her chin protectively.

"What'll it be, ma'am, a dishwasher, a hostess, maybe a server or two? No, wait, you already *have* all of those! Looking for more employees to steal away from me?" he asked, walking toward her with a cold smile. He lit a cigarette, despite the no smoking law that had gone into effect at the beginning of the summer. His dark brown hair was perfectly styled as usual, and his fashionable day old stubble looked more like two days today. He wore a sharp navy dress shirt tucked into a pair of belted dark pants with black leather shoes, and she smelled the infamous cologne. He made a point of inspecting her as well, looking her up and down, taking in her loose soft peasant blouse and the short denim skirt she wore, his eyes lingering especially on her legs.

She looked him in the eyes. "Actually, they've been coming to me in droves," she shot back in her throaty voice as he closed his eyes to take a drag off his cigarette, seeming to listen to her speak.

"Sit down…please," he said, gesturing to the chair she had just left. He sat at the same table, watching her carefully as she arranged herself in the seat and crossed her legs, brown from summer days on the beach with Tyson, she reminded herself, screaming at herself inside for being here. This was so wrong. What was she thinking? His large, heavily lashed brown eyes were intense on her blue ones as he puffed again on the cigarette.

"So…if you're not here to steal my staff, then why are you here?" he asked, smiling beguilingly at her.

She wondered the same question herself, but she was determined not to let him see it. She let her eyelids drop for effect and took a slow, nonchalant breath. "Oh, I was just wondering what's going on over here. You know, if people are leaving and coming over to my side, I figure there must be something to it. I'd like to know what's going on," she said as coolly as she could manage, swinging her leg absently. He noticed her legs again and smiled, enjoying the sight, which sent a strange chill down her spine. She stopped swinging her leg, casually tugging her skirt toward her knees.

"I think it's just the changing of the guard, you know; end of summer?" he said lightly, flicking his ash onto the table. She watched in disgust. The server with the beard appeared with an ashtray, a bottle of Amstel Light, and a chilled glass. Rick poured the cold amber liquid slowly down the inside of the glass. "Anything for you, love?"

"Maybe a water," she said to the waiter, knowing she wouldn't be staying long enough to drink it. But it was just conversation. She felt strangely guarded. It was a familiar feeling, and she realized she had acted this way around him for many years—not herself at all, but just playing a role, wondering what would be happening in the next scene.

"No wine?" he said, mildly amused.

"No, thank you," she said firmly. When he smirked, she added, "It's early still. I have to work."

"Ah, yes, you're busy at The Sound Side."

"Yes, *we are*," she said accenting the "we."

He stared at her chest and laughed again, taking another drag of the cigarette, "So enlighten me, please," he sniffed. "Why exactly are you here?"

"I just want to know what's going on. Why can't you pay your staff? Is your coke habit getting in your way?" she continued, seeming unable to stop herself. "Are you going to close this place?" she asked, suddenly brave, suddenly wanting to get to the core of the problem.

He raised his eyebrows, curled his lips into a smirk, and laughed through this nose. "So what have they been telling you?"

"Not a whole lot, other than they haven't been getting paid and they need to eat," she said. Her comment hung in the air like a storm cloud.

He smoked some more and then ground out the cigarette in the ashtray. He ran a hand through his hair and looked to the side. "Well, I guess some of that's true. I have a lot of overhead here. But let me ask you this: why the hell would *you* care?"

She shrugged, "Curiosity. You're a good business man. Your business is too good to go to the dogs…or so I thought," she said, trying to meet his eyes. He was suddenly evasive, but her blue eyes were relentless and he caught himself looking at her.

"Times are tough. I think you know that," he said quietly.

"Yes, they are. And that's why you bust your *ass* trying to do everything possible to keep yourself afloat…and everybody else who works for you. What are you doing, Rick? You're about to go under. You're not still doing cocaine? Not with your baby at home?" She could feel her eyes boring into his, and this time, he was the one who was off guard.

He did not look at her as he took a large gulp of his beer. "Look, this is my business. You don't need to barge in here and start asking questions. What the hell?"

She shook her head. "I don't know why I'm here either, if you want to know the truth. It's not my business," she said curtly and picked up her purse, preparing to leave. He reached out and placed his hand over hers.

"I'm sorry. I'm being rude. Stay a minute, will you?"

She looked at him, shocked, as if he had turned into someone else before her eyes. She sat back down. "So…?" He released her hand after an uncomfortable moment.

"I *have* been doing some coke…a lot of coke lately. But I can handle it. I'm not addicted."

"What about Torie and Ellie?" she asked softly, trying to get him to look at her.

"She took Ellie. They're at her mother's in Virginia Beach."

"When?"

"She's been there for about a month now. She's not coming back," he said to the wall.

"Are you going up there? You can start over. Your dad will help you out, so you can start over up there."

He shook his head. "No. No. This one's on me. He's done with me, too. I'm in debt up to my eyeballs. I screwed it up…again. I don't learn, you know? It's just a matter of time before I fold this place," he said, draining the beer glass. He looked at her, vulnerable this time. She was no longer playing a role. Their eyes met. She had not seen him this way for a long, long time.

"You can change it, Rick. Don't let it beat you. You're looking in all the wrong places."

He tapped his fingertips on the table and looked around.

"I'm working on it. I know everything I've done wrong. Just tell me something…what did *he* do right?" he asked her, anguish in his voice.

She was not prepared for this question and floundered for the right frame of mind to tell him. "Tyson?"

He nodded.

She swallowed. How could she tell him, of all people, how she felt about Tyson Garrett? "He…he gives me everything he has. He loves me more than life. He reads my mind, my soul…he knows me inside and out…he makes me laugh, he takes care of me. I can't keep my hands off of him," she laughed gently in spite of herself. "He's the father of my child," she said, poignantly, watching for Rick's reaction.

His eyes flew open wide and his face began to melt. He looked down at her stomach. His large brown eyes gazed into hers and he looked at her hopelessly. "I'm glad for you, Stacie," he finally said. He sighed deeply and cast his eyes around. His fingers tapped nervously on the table again before he ran them into his hair, leaving tufts of it sticking up between his fingers like paintbrushes. "Do you…even remember ever *loving me?*" he asked.

She felt a pang of loss, the old sad feeling she used to have before she finally gave up hope that they would ever make it. It was an old memory, but suddenly, she remembered it as if it were just yesterday. She remembered his sweet brown eyes when they first met, and the way he treated her a long time ago. She remembered caring. He watched her carefully, as if waiting for her to drive the dagger in. "Yeah. I do, Rick."

"I'm so sorry I hurt you, Stacie," he said. "I was such an idiot. I still am.

Can you forgive me?"

She was surprised and thought a moment. Here, surely, was why she had really come. But could she forgive him, after it was all said and done? After all the hurt and resentment, after all he had taken from her. Then she nodded slowly. The reason became suddenly apparent. She swallowed. "I do forgive you. But you need to make it right with Torie. You have a *child*, Rick, a family. You should give yourself a second chance. Don't give up on yourself. Don't give up on them. Fight for them. Make it happen. You'll always lose if you keep letting yourself."

Later that evening at The Sound Side, she stood at the end of the kitchen line, watching Tyson and Bobby, the new sous-chef, as they put meals together companionably, laughing and talking, calling to the servers and tapping the bell when the orders were up. Tyson looked at her from time to time, assessing her expression, probably wondering why she was so attentive all evening. She didn't want her meeting with Rick to be an issue on his birthday, so she wanted to get the conversation over with as soon as possible. Tyson watched her as she appeared from time to time, obviously trying to get his attention. During a momentary lull in business, he wiped his hands on his apron and entered her office, where she sat, curled up on the sofa, waiting for him. As he sat beside her in his white apron, she curled herself into him, taking his hands in hers and kissing him.

"What have you done? Don't tell me you ran over my cat!" he laughed at her guilty expression, then kissed her and stroked her face. She looked at him shamefully. "Damn, are you having an affair?" he asked her seriously, making her laugh.

"No! Never! Like I'd *ever* have the time!" she said and pulled his face closer into hers and kissed him passionately. "I feel so...*sick*! I went to see Rick today."

He looked confused.

"I know it's weird. You know how I told you Father Jack asked me if I'd forgiven Rick?" she asked, taking his hand and threading her fingers through his. He nodded tentatively. "So I went over to Pompano's today. I passed it three times before I went in. I talked to him about his business and what he's doing. He's using coke and Torie left him. He's in a lot of debt. And then he asked me if...I remembered ever *loving him?*" Tears began to roll down her cheeks as Tyson stared at her for a moment.

"He asked me what it is you do right, why I love you so much, and I told him. I told him I'm having your baby. And he asked me to forgive him," she said, sniffing, pressing her fingertips to her eyes and looking into his, feeling as if she had betrayed him. She waited for his rebuke. She waited to see his eyes cloud over and for the rant to start. Instead, he looked carefully at her and took her hand again.

"Did you forgive him?" he asked. When she was silent, he continued. "That was why you went there, right? To forgive him? Did you?" he asked her softly, gazing at her intently.

"Yes," she whispered.

He stroked the back of her hand with his fingers. "Then...what's the problem?"

A wave of guilt washed over her. "I'm so *mad* at Father Jack right now!" she said sharply, wiping her eyes again. "But this is on me. It's my doing. I just didn't ever want to go there again. I thought I had it all worked out. Forgiving is one thing, but forgetting is the hard part. He asked me if I remembered ever loving him. *And I do.* I told him that..." she said, more tears pouring from her eyes, steeling herself for his anger, his jealousy. "I thought all these emotions were gone. The love I once felt a long time ago. But it's like it's back; it's way down in there somewhere, and I don't know what to do with it. I don't want to remember any of it anymore. I just want *us*..." she whispered, her voice thick with tears.

The shadow of a smile played at the corners of his lips, and she thought she saw the dimples in his cheeks. He looked at her with his clear green eyes. "You know what I think?"

She shook her head, honestly.

"I think your heart is big enough to hold all of us," he said, threading his fingers through hers again. "You can handle this. It's fine. Just so long as *I* have the biggest place in there…I'm okay with it. That's why I love you, Stacie. Only you could love Rick. You're nothing but love."

She pulled his face into hers with both of her hands and kissed him desperately.

September 23rd was a special day, beyond the first day of fall. She fixed Tyson breakfast in bed for his birthday, French toast with pepper bacon, orange juice, and coffee. Mojo sat at the foot of the bed, tail twitching, observing from a safe distance. It was difficult to buy gifts for a man who had everything he wanted and valued material possessions so little. She had upgraded his phone so he could have Internet access at his fingertips, and he seemed genuinely pleased. She had found an autographed copy of *The Killer Angels* months ago at a used bookstore, which he loved. He unwrapped the gifts in the bed after she had taken away the breakfast tray. He finished his party with what he told her he really wanted, *her*, and they walked on the beach later before they went in to work.

At dinner, she had planned a surprise party for him in the dining room, and unbeknownst to him, she had arranged for Bobby, the new cook, to take over the dinner service for the rest of the evening. When she told Tyson he had customers who wished to give their compliments to the chef, and he emerged into the dining room, the party welcomed him to the table, shouting, "Surprise!" and seated him in their midst. He looked truly surprised and kissed her on the cheek, telling her he was touched and thanking her. But when he noticed Jesse and Mel in the middle of the group, his mouth fell open in astonishment. "Oh, my God!" he laughed and looked at Stacie, amazed. "How did you pull this off?"

"We've been keeping up by email and decided it would be so much fun to surprise you!" she said, smiling widely at him, then at them, glad that they had been able to give him something special. "They'll be staying a couple of days with us," she laughed as he shook his head and went to embrace his brother and sister-in-law. He grinned so broadly that she thought she hadn't seen him this happy in awhile.

He had lots of presents to open, and he seemed slightly embarrassed being the center of attention. His mother had sent a loaf of her homemade bread by Jesse and Mel and he breathed in deeply its aroma. They gave him a basket with a tag that read, "Bloody Mary Survival Kit" with all the fixings for Jesse's famous Bloody Marys that Tyson raved about. There was a nice sports watch from Shelly and more books and wine from the Murphys and the Colemans, a CD from Andrew, and a special bottle of Vodka from Zack and Nina, who had come over briefly to join the party. Bets had made his favorite coconut birthday cake for him. Shelly snapped pictures of everyone at the table and took one of Tyson and Stacie. Stacie watched him enjoying himself and felt her heart swell. He was always the one doing things for other people, so it was nice seeing him get some well-deserved attention.

Tyson was glad to have Jesse and Mel at their house. He and Stacie took them to the Wright Brothers' museum, called the Wright Memorial, and the Chicamacomico life saving station in Rodanthe. These were places they had not had time to visit on their first trip down. Tyson knew with Jesse's love of boats that he would appreciate seeing the life saving station. And it wouldn't be a proper trip to the Outer Banks without breakfast at Sam and Omie's! Jesse and Mel ventured to the Hatteras lighthouse on their own after breakfast, while Tyson and Stacie worked, and later that evening, witnessed the sunset on top of Jockey's Ridge on their way back, as Stacie had suggested.

Days later, after Jesse and Mel had gone home, Stacie stood in the empty dining room. She checked her watch. It was 2:30 p.m. and she was waiting for Erin Gray, her friend and former employee, now the caterer who would be providing the wedding dinner. Erin breezed in wearing jeans, a T-shirt, and a cardigan, her short dark hair a bit disheveled from the wind. They greeted each other with a hug, and Erin apologized for her attire. "I have to take Matthew to swimming lessons after this. Usually I dress more professionally."

"Nonsense, you look great! How is everyone?"

"Great! Matt said to tell you hello and that he's really looking forward to your big event."

Stacie laughed, "You mean the first of a double header!"

"I know! Congratulations!" Erin exclaimed, glancing at Stacie's stomach. "You're not even showing," she said.

"It's the loose clothes. I guess I'll have to break down and get some of those jeans with the stretch panel-thing here soon," Stacie said, indicating where the stretch panel would go on the maternity jeans she had thought about buying.

"God, I hated being pregnant. I hurled for eight months straight. But it agrees with you!"

Stacie smiled, feeling the odd tug in her stomach she'd had all morning. "Well, let's check this out. What do you think you can do with this room to make it look like a wedding?"

"Oh, there's great possibility here. I envision white linen table clothes and glass bowls with floating camellias from your friend Sue…and lots of candles. We'll do the hors d'oeuvres table over there," she said, waving her hand to the far side of the room. "We'll set up the buffet here by the kitchen. And we'll have our bartender at the bar so Zack and Andrew can have some fun. Are you still planning on one hundred people?"

Stacie nodded, feeling a sharper pain, but trying to hide it. They sat at one of the tables and went over the menus they had discussed over their previous emails. Erin took a brief tour of the kitchen again before leaving, excited that the plans were exactly the way she had envisioned.

Stacie sat in the office on the couch, sliding her fingers down the sides of her cell phone and flipping it over, absently, doing it again and again. She stared at the map of the Outer Banks on the wall of her office and the picture of Tyson and herself from his birthday, in a frame on her desk. She checked her watch again. Four o'clock. He would be there shortly, and she would have to tell him she would be leaving. The radio was playing and she heard him bang through the back door, singing along with Eric Clapton's "Layla." She heard him knocking around in the kitchen, probably putting on his apron, washing his hands at the sink, and then his beautiful face appeared at the door. One look at her changed his sunny smile to a look of concern in just an instant. He was at her side on the couch, taking her hand, while her other hand continued to slide down the phone and flip it over.

"What's going on, baby?" he said low in her ear, kissing her lips and caressing the side of her face. His green eyes searched hers frantically.

"There's some blood…more blood than I want to see. I've called Karen, and she wants me to come in and let her check me," she said stoically.

He swallowed. "Okay. Do you want to go now? We'll take my truck."

"No. I can go over there by myself. You can stay."

"No fucking way. I'm taking you. Don't worry about tonight. Bobby's got it. I'll call him right now. He's probably on his way this minute."

His devotion moved her. She placed her cool hand on the side of his jaw and he closed his eyes, pulling her close. She felt the muscle in his jaw working, and she knew he was gearing himself up to be ready for the worst. She was doing the same thing. And then he set her away from him, working his fingertips over the touch screen on his phone, placing the call to Bobby, walking out of her office to speak to him discreetly. She stood and collected her purse, glancing again at their picture on her desk, feeling a burst of love for him again. She found him in the kitchen, hanging the apron back on the hook and fishing car keys out of his pocket. They heard tires crunching in the parking lot, and before she could finish sliding on her lip gloss, Bobby was there, looking concerned. He wished them well, and they were out the back door.

Stacie slung her purse over her shoulder and felt herself being swept up in the air by Tyson's strong arms. "Oh, for God's sake, Ty!" she laughed and looked at him. He sniffed and she saw a tear at the corner of his eye. Her breath caught and she sighed audibly. "Oh…Ty…it's going to be fine," she whispered, murmuring his mantra. She wiped the tear away, and kissing his neck, clung to him as he carried her to the Chevy truck in the parking lot.

She awoke in the lamp-lit bedroom later, stretching in her bed, smelling a heavenly aroma coming from the kitchen. He moved his book aside and reached over from behind to touch her, rubbing her back, and pulling her close to him. She felt Mojo stretch at her feet as well, and she turned to look at Tyson. "How long have I been asleep?" she asked, wiping her mouth with the back of her hand.

"A couple of hours. You needed it." He held her again and kissed the back of her neck. "Karen said you've got to slow down."

"I remember. But everything's okay. It was just some spotting." She remembered Karen ordering her to take a few days off, and no sex for a couple of days either, which saddened her, but she would suck it up and be big about it. She pulled his hand across her to rest underneath her chin, and she felt him nestle closer to her.

"There's shrimp and grits in the oven," he said, stroking her face tenderly.

They ate by candlelight in the kitchen. He looked at her, concern etched deep in his face. "You dodged a bullet today," he said seriously. She had not heard him talk to her this way before. It was almost fatherly. She nodded and savored the food. He continued quietly, "You've got to stop trying to do it all, Stacie. I know we have a lot on our plate right now, but it's time to take this seriously. Let everybody else pick up the ball. No more parties till the wedding. And you're only working four or five hours a day, starting in two days."

"You're laying down the law?" she teased, knowing he was serious.

"Damn right I am. I know you're playing right now. But I'm serious. You have to take better care of yourself. I feel like I'm trying to catch the damn *wind* in a jar, taking care of you."

She met his earnest gaze and wanted to cry. He was so precious to her. She covered his hand with hers on the kitchen table. "I'll do better," she murmured, knowing it was an inept reply to his words, and how she felt about him.

"Don't make this hard. I'm on it. But you *have* to do your part."

"I will. I promise. It'll be me and Mojo, hanging out at home."

"Good," he said, winking at her and taking her plate.

Shelly stopped by the next day, fresh from the doctor to show off her foot, finally free of its cast. Stacie met her at the foot of her porch stairs and they walked slowly across the boardwalk to sit on the beach. It was the first of October, and they had the beach to themselves except for one or two walkers in long-sleeved shirts and floppy hats. The sky was a brilliant blue, and gulls flew energetically in circles above them, laughing and calling to one another.

Stacie gathered her hair into a messy bun as Shelly talked excitedly about the events of the day. "If this had been my driving foot, I'd never have been able to do what I've done, going to work, and taking care of myself. I'm just so glad that thing is off!" she exclaimed, removing her soft boot and rubbing her foot gingerly.

Stacie felt guilty. "I'm sorry I haven't been much help to you lately," she said.

"It's okay. I haven't needed it! All I really need is your company. I'm so glad *you're* finally taking care of yourself. Tyson was fit to be tied with you for a while there."

"I know. What if our kid is like *me*? The poor guy....Do you think he'll be able to handle the two of us?" she smiled, but she felt concern for him just the same.

"I'm sure he's preparing himself for the worst!" Shelly said, wryly.

"So what's this earth-shattering news you have to tell me about that I'm not going to believe?" asked Stacie curiously.

Shelly was beside herself with an expression of wonder on her face. "I put an offer on a beach house today."

"Good! It's about time. We've got people coming to stay in it in three weeks!"

"It won't be a problem. The guy's really motivated to close the deal and get out. You won't believe this," she said breathlessly, watching Stacie's face intently. "It's *Rick's house*!" she dropped her bomb effectively as Stacie absorbed the news in silent shock.

"What?" she finally said, blinking at her sister. "Rick is selling his *house?*"

"Mm-hmm and his BMW...*and* the boat. He's doing everything he can to keep the restaurant afloat. He's cut the staff back to bare bones, all the ones who didn't leave already. He's cut the menu. Don't be surprised if you hear he's sleeping there."

"Oh, my God!" Stacie whispered. "I just can't believe this. How is the house? Is it a pigsty? Torie's been gone a while now. It's got to be trashed."

"I guess he had somebody clean it…or maybe he did it himself, but it looks pretty good. I heard he's been going up to Virginia Beach and visiting her."

"Is she going to take him back?" Stacie whispered.

"Jeanna said it all depends on how long he can hold it together, and if he can keep the business open."

"Of course, if there's nowhere to stay when she comes back, and all the toys are gone, I guess maybe she'll be rethinking it…."

"Well, that's another way I come in. I'll be helping him find a rental property. It has to be the cheapest thing on the beach with two bedrooms, he said. He's driving a '98 Honda Civic."

"Oh, I just can't believe this! He would never have been caught *dead* in a car like that before! So, you're actually working with him?" Stacie asked incredulously.

"I will be. Jeanna's been talking with him to this point, but he'll be working with me after we close the deal next week."

"Does he know you're my sister? Surely he remembers you! I mean, how weird is that for him, and for you!" Stacie exclaimed, raking back escaped strands of hair against the breeze.

"Yeah. Jeanna said he was taking it about like you are right now, but at this point he just needs our services, and he's not acting too proud to beg, so to speak."

Stacie shook her head yet again in disbelief. "Of all the small world stories!" she whispered.

"What do you think Tyson will think of this?" Shelly asked warily.

"Oh, he won't care. He'll think it's funny, probably…but we're *not* telling any of the family they're staying at *Rick's house*! It's too weird!"

"Okay, but there's just one thing you've got to promise me?"

"What?" asked Stacie, ready for another bombshell.

"Kyle is never supposed to know I've bought this place. I'm doing this as an investment for him. Tyson and I have talked about this at length, and I think it's the best way to go right now, with the economy. This kind of beach property is still holding its value over other investments. I want to be able to give him something when the time is right. He deserves a break, and when he's ready to settle down, I want to be able to give him something substantial. Stu and I always talked about the time when he would take over the business, and when that fell apart, I had to have a back-up plan. I just want it to be a secret, in case I lose money on it and have to come up with something else."

Stacie nodded, a slow smile forming around the corners of her mouth. "I think that's a wonderful idea. Kyle's going to do you really proud one day. I can't think of a better way to reveal Stu's legacy to him. That's one secret I think you'd be smart to keep."

"Exactly! See, I'm learning," Shelly beamed at her.

Stacie smiled back at her sister, but looked at her pensively, thinking about Rick and their conversation at the restaurant. "Aren't we all?"

Chapter 12

TYING THE KNOT

Indian summer ushered in the weekend of Tyson and Stacie's wedding. The late October sky was a delightful bright blue without clouds or wind, and the air was fresh and crisp. The families had arrived almost as the movers had squealed out of the driveway, and new linens had been thrown upon beds. Shelly and her team—Rob, Jeanna, and for one hour each day as Tyson had allowed, Stacie—had placed dishes in the cabinets, towels in the bathrooms, and a coffeemaker on the kitchen counter. What more could they possibly need? Breathless from the preparations, Stacie traipsed up the stairs with Dan and Elaine in tow with what little luggage they had brought for the occasion. Stacie looked around again, unable to shake the odd feeling she had, knowing Rick and his family, for whom he had dumped her, once lived here. She steeled herself again, and in spite of her feelings, grinned boldly at her mother.

"Now you leave the rest to me," Elaine told her firmly, placing a hand on Stacie's arm, and after regarding Shelly's ankle boot, giving her a warning glance. "You girls have worn yourselves to a frazzle getting this place together. Let me take care of the Garretts. We're buddies now, you know, so I can get them settled in, and we'll plan on meeting you at the church tonight for the rehearsal." Her eyes twinkled at Stacie as she asked, "So, who all is coming?"

"Wade and Connie, of course, Mel and Jesse, and Henry," she smiled back at her fashionable-looking mother and Shelly.

"I wondered if he'd make an appearance after all that *drama* he pulled back in the summer!" Elaine quipped, rearranging her silver-blonde hair from the effects of the sea breeze.

"Well…Tyson was a little surprised too. We think it's because of that girl he met when he was here. He asked Ty if he could bring her. Her name is Sandy, with an X—short for Alexandra." Shelly rolled her eyes. "Whatever…she's coming up from Carolina, and she's planning to be here for the weekend."

"*Here?*" Elaine screeched, indicating the house, and looking horrified.

"Oh, no! Her parents have a place on the beach somewhere, so she'll be staying there. So will Henry, probably. I doubt you'll be seeing much of him," Stacie laughed.

"Oh, that's *so tacky!*" her mother said, disapproval written on her face.

"That's Henry!" Stacie nodded. "Anyway, at least he's here. Tyson never expected that much."

"And Chelsea will be bringing Kyle in tomorrow night after the game. Just in time for the reception," said Shelly, eyes sparkling. It had been over a month since she had seen him.

"We'll be so glad to see them both! Dan and I will take him back up to school on Sunday," Elaine reminded her. Then she changed the subject, looking around the bright and airy beach house.

"Well…this place is just lovely! Everything looks nice and clean."

"Thanks!" Shelly said, winking at Stacie. "There hasn't been time to decorate just yet, but you should all be comfortable at least."

Dan puffed in the front door with the cooler from their car. "Nice digs, Bones!" he bellowed to Shelly, using his longtime nickname for her, setting down the cooler and pushing up his glasses. "And how are you, Cool Breeze?" he asked, giving equal time to Stacie, taking them both in a large bear-hug. "Ready for your big day?" he beamed at the bride-to-be.

"Oh, Daddy, it's all great; just a little redundant, don't you think?"

"What? Nonsense! We're not having any negative talk when you're about to get hitched to such a fine catch as Tyson." Her father looked at her with his intuitive eyes. "Maybe you didn't know this, but Tyson came to us the night of your birthday party and asked your mom and me for our blessing."

Stacie gasped and glanced at her mother who was beaming along with Shelly. "No, I didn't know that," she said softly, feeling humbled.

"This is all going to be *fantastic*! I hope you'll enjoy every minute of it," Dan remarked.

"I know, and I will, Daddy. I guess I'm just a little tired," she said to her father, her all-time biggest cheerleader and supporter.

"That's *totally* understandable, darling," her mother crooned as they sat down on the new sofas in the large gathering room. "How have you been feeling?"

"Fine, really. Tyson's been keeping a tight rein on me. I'm glad there's so much to do; otherwise I'd be bored to death!"

Stacie regretted saying anything negative. Of course, she felt nothing but blessed. But it felt almost mundane, the thought of dressing up and walking down the aisle in front of everyone who already knew how they were. And with a baby already on the way, it seemed almost…*absurd*! Still she knew she shouldn't dampen anyone's spirits. Tyson was certainly thrilled about the whole thing, as much as a man can get into a wedding. All their friends and family were truly delighted for them both, and a little put out that they wouldn't accept gifts. She beamed at her father, promising herself she would do a better job of being enthusiastic. The weather was certainly doing its part to create good karma. She sighed pleasantly. If there *were* one negative thing, it was that she and Tyson had been so busy they seemed to pass like ships in the night, both too exhausted to do anything more than kiss one another goodnight.

Draped in her digital camera, Kristen Dunleavy, the wedding photographer, was the first person to greet Stacie at the chapel. As the others milled about on the wrap-around seaside deck, enjoying the warm weather, Kristen shook back her shiny hair against the breeze and had Stacie pose in the chapel doorway for a portrait in her creamy dress, her pale hair blowing loosely around her face. Stacie attempted to steal a glance inside to see whether Tyson were there. She had seen his truck in the lot when she had let Shelly off at the door, and she figured he was tied up with his family and possibly Father Jack inside at the moment.

"Would you like to have a picture with Tyson?" Kristen asked intuitively, picking up on her thoughts. When Stacie nodded, she took charge of the situation and paged him from the chapel. He was there in a flash, sharply dressed in a crisp Oxford shirt tucked into khaki pants, which caused Stacie to inhale sharply and break into a smile.

When he saw her, he did the same. Taking her hand, he pulled her in close and murmured into her hair. "Mm, there you are!" he breathed, and then to Kristen he said, "I see you've met my girlfriend!" She snapped a picture of them together. She then asked Stacie to drape her arm across his shoulder, showing the sparkling diamond ring, and feigned shock at the stone, causing them to laugh appropriately for the photo. Two more shots were clicked off, and then they were inside the chapel, getting down to business, listening to Father Jack and following directions mechanically, Tyson winking at her playfully from time to time.

He commandeered her elbow after the rehearsal and escorted her quickly to the truck, telling his father they would meet them at the restaurant for the rehearsal dinner. "I'm sorry. Was it too rude to drag you off like that?" he asked, looking abashed. Then, frustrated, he explained, "It's just that I haven't had a minute with you in about three days. I need a fiancée fix in a really bad way!" he growled into her ear, tucking her into the truck's passenger seat. He helped her take her seatbelt and kissed her before making his way to the other side.

"You're sweet. I've missed you too," she said, taking his hand as soon as he had pulled out into the road, heading north to The Croatan Inn, where they would all converge for cocktails and dinner. He smiled as he drove, the breeze from his half-opened window blowing her hair. He noticed and raised it.

"Did you feed Mojo?" he asked absently. When he saw her mortified look, he reacted with a sigh and rolled his eyes.

"Of course I fed him," she laughed. "But I did *not touch* the litter box!"

"Good! That's off limits for you," he said, smirking at her, good-naturedly. "Pregnant women aren't supposed to be near that stuff."

"Ah, yes, the pregnant, forty-year-old bride-to-be…practicing baby care on a cat!" she derided herself.

"Enough already!" he laughed, looking at her sideways. "What's got you on edge?"

She shook her head and took in glimpses of the ocean as they drove along. She sighed, "I don't know. I seem to be the only one who thinks all of this is just a little bit weird, you know?"

"Well, just keep your thoughts to yourself. You're killing my buzz right now," he smiled and gazed at her just long enough to be safe before returning his eyes to the road. "You're right, though. No one else thinks it's weird."

"Okay then," she murmured, tightening her hold on his brown hand in her lap. After a moment she asked him, "So…are the men folk taking you out on the town for the proverbial *bachelor party*?"

"Ahh, *that's* it. You're worried about me going out and defiling myself before the wedding day?" He laughed silently, watching the road.

"Yep, while I stay home curled up like a good girl with the cat."

He thought a moment. "Nah. I think I'll pass. The only one I want to be with tonight is you."

"But it's tradition, right? A rite of passage, so to speak. What if they twist your arm? And they've come all this *way*! There's no way you won't be going," she provoked him, batting her eyes.

"It's not like I'm twenty-four or five, you know? I think our situation's a little different. Don't try to start something, okay?" he met her dubious look as they pulled into the parking lot, truck tires crunching over crushed shells.

The dinner was boisterous and jovial without any trouble. Stacie enjoyed watching Xandy gravitating close to Henry, who looked equally uncomfortable with the people with whom he had failed to bond. Xandy seemed lovely, a slight, blonde girl with pinkish-fair skin and deep blue eyes. Her smile showed incredible teeth that were doubtlessly the result of excellent orthodontic work. Her diamond studs were almost the size of Shelly's, causing Stacie to stare more than once.

The two families had definitely become "buddies" as Elaine had claimed. Shelly and Mel had helped the mothers put together a video montage of the couple, from babyhood to the present, and Stacie had joked that the show promised to be as long as *Gone With the Wind*. Jesse quipped that there would be an intermission after the teenage years so people would have a chance to stretch their legs. After a toast or two, it was time to wrap things up, and the boys, as Stacie had predicted, invited Tyson out for one last evening to celebrate bachelorhood. She winked at Tyson and urged him to go.

"But—don't expect me to pick you up and drag you into the house if you're stinking drunk. And no throwing up in the bed either," she said, laying down the law. "On second thought, why don't you just stay at the house with all of them and leave me in peace," she said, grinning. "I'll see you at the altar tomorrow!" Tyson kissed her guiltily before being swept away by his brother.

"All right, dude! You just got the green light. Let's go!" exclaimed Jesse, wrapping his arm around Tyson's neck and giving Stacie a quick peck on the cheek. "I promise we'll take good care of him," he said, winking at her.

"Oh, I have no doubt about *that!*" she said, wryly, going to Shelly's car for her lift home.

Around one o'clock, she heard him knocking around in the bathroom, flushing the toilet and brushing his teeth. She felt Mojo being relocated to the foot of the bed, and Tyson's cool body slipping in behind her under the covers.

"Are you Mrs. Garrett?" he asked liquidly in her ear. Assessing that he wasn't too far gone, she giggled as he wrapped his arm around her, smelling like beer. "The boys who dropped me off here said you could show me a real good time. I'm just checking to make sure I'm in the right place!" he whispered and pulled her around to kiss him.

At five bells on Saturday, Dr. Dan Edmonds, with misty eyes, presented his arm for Stacie. They stood in the narthex of the little chapel, the waning afternoon light slanting through watery-looking hand-blown glass windows. Kristen snapped pictures of them together. Stacie's father looked dashing in his black suit and silver hair. The organist was coming to the end of the Trumpet Voluntary. Stacie stood beside her father, smoothing the ivory silk pleats of her dress, as he returned her bouquet of creamy roses and green hydrangea, tied with a green ribbon. She checked; her hair was still holding its own in an elegant loose twist. She studied the diamond on her finger, seeing its rainbows reflecting on the wall of the narthex. She thought of Chelsea and Kyle on the road after the football game

UVA had apparently won. Finally, she looked up and watched as Shelly made her way gingerly down the short aisle in her lovely pale green dress to take her place to the left of Father Jack, who was looking exceptionally huge and joyful right now. The music changed. And then she saw him.

Tyson Garrett, taller-looking and dark, stunning in his dark suit and green tie, setting off his hot green eyes like peridots, stood at the altar beside his father. As he looked up and saw her, his gaze became molten on hers, and she saw the dimples begin to form at each end of his growing smile. She saw his lips form the word, "Wow." And then she knew—she knew what they were doing was the most incredible thing two people in love could ever do to solidify their journey together. Her love for him ignited again from deep within her, and she felt her breath catch as she hesitated for a moment before taking that first step with her father toward the man she loved with all her heart and soul. She trembled and felt her flowers vibrating as they strolled down the aisle, Dan checking her face every other moment, enjoying her expressions. She gave him a little smile and a wink as they stopped at the altar steps, and then she was riveted to Tyson, so like his own father beside him, smiling at her too, a prediction of the man with whom she would be growing old. It was reassuring and comforting, glancing at Connie and her parents, knowing what she and Tyson could become and all that was in store for them. Surely, people were there watching all this, but she was suddenly completely unaware of them, looking only at *him,* feeling the sensual touch of his hand as he accepted hers from her father. She felt a vague flutter for the first time inside her and gasped, wishing she could tell him that she had just felt their child move. He watched her eyes flash and squeezed her hand, wondering.

She floated with him up the two stairs to the altar and joined Father Jack with Shelly and Wade as the ceremony began. She must have said the prayers, repeated her vows, lit the candle, and accepted the blessings, but all she could think about was his glorious face in front of her, the pressure of his hand under her elbow, guiding her back and forth into place. He slid the ring on her finger and she did the same to his. Then finally, they were in each other's arms and he was kissing her, like he had never kissed her before. There was applause, and when they were being introduced by Father Jack as Mr. and Mrs. Tyson Garrett, they beamed at each other with joy. More organ music pealed forth. Shelly handed her the bouquet she hadn't realized she'd given her. When she turned, she saw them all: her exuberant mother and father and all the Garretts, and Xandy, all looking fine and happy. Her friends were there: the Murphys, the Colemans, and the Brantleys with little Allie dressed like a princess in pink, Karen Walters with her husband and teenage daughter, Zack, Nina, Andrew, Ava, Tom and Liz Davenport, Tyson's friends from New Jersey, her college roommate, Tina, and her family…all the lights in her life. A tear slid down the side of her radiant face as she took her husband's arm and let him guide her back down the aisle.

Kristen was waiting for them outside the chapel with her camera, holding up her hand to snap their picture yet again. They stopped for a moment. Then Tyson held up his hand, saying, "Can you give us just a minute?" He continued guiding Stacie out the church doors and into the fading afternoon light and the sea breeze. When they were away, he drew her up in his arms and sighed contentedly in her ear. "You are one beautiful bride. I love you so much," he murmured. "I can't believe you're my wife!" He kissed her again.

When he released her, she glanced around for others and said quickly, "When you took my hand at the altar, I felt the baby move for the first time!"

His green eyes got as large as she had ever seen them. "Oh, my God!" he whispered in awe before he reached for her stomach reflexively. He looked up at her expectantly. "Have you felt it again?"

She shook her head. "Not yet. I guess it was the excitement. I thought it was butterflies at first."

"So you *are* excited about all this after all."

"Oh, Ty, of course I am," she said, stroking the side of his face. "I've never been this happy in my life!" They heard a click and realized that Kristen was back, doing her job; they turned and smiled for her again. She zoomed in on their hands, catching a nice shot of their wedding rings against the black and ivory of their garments. Stacie felt herself sigh as they were whisked away to the side door of the church with Wade and Shelly laughing behind them. After the usual pictures in front of the altar with Father Jack and the families, they were ushered to the seaside deck for a few more before heading over to The Sound Side in Stacie's car.

Stacie felt as if she were floating all the way there, and her face never lost its smile as she glanced repeatedly at her handsome husband, driving her car. The parking lot was as full as it would usually be on a summer Saturday night, and she was moved to think all these people were here just for them, to celebrate the big step they had just taken. The rose-colored sun was setting on the sound beyond the high pitched roof, and happily, she noticed Kristen at the parking lot's edge, capturing the image with her camera.

They stood for a moment taking it all in before they headed to the steps to join the throng of their guests. The scene inside took Stacie's breath away. Candlelight glimmered at all the tables, which had been covered with white linen tablecloths and set with large glass bowls filled with floating camellias of various shades of red, rose, and palest pink. The scent of women's perfume and men's cologne mingled satisfyingly with the food's aromas. She had never seen a more distinguished-looking crowd in her place. The combination of all the colorful women's dresses with the men's elegant suits made the décor complete and breathtaking. Tyson shared her feeling of awe and looked at her with his crinkling green eyes and a smile full of wonder. He did not drop her hand and tended to pull her close to him as people saw they had arrived. "I'm not letting you go," he murmured. "You're way too hot to share tonight. Besides, you're mine now!" he said, winking at her.

She tried to take it all in. Erin and Matt, the caterers, waved at them from near the kitchen door. Music played from the sound system; she took in the South Street band, setting up on the stage, gasping at their changed appearances as well. Sugar Fisher, who usually sang in jeans and an island shirt and flip-flops, was a vision in a bright red dress that hugged every previously undisclosed curve she had. Tyson, eyebrows raised, shared Stacie's reaction to her as well. When Sugar looked over, Stacie licked her finger and held it in the air, making the sound of steam, "Tss!" and Sugar laughed, shaking her head.

Elaine, in beaded avocado silk, was at their side in a moment with Dan at her elbow, claiming hugs, followed by Connie in a beautiful copper-colored dress. Wade had separated her from Tyson at this point to gather his son in a warm embrace that sent more tears down Stacie's cheeks. When he took her in his arms next, she noticed he was crying as well. "We're so happy for you both!" Wade exclaimed. "This is such a blessing for all of us. Welcome to the Garrett family," he said and gave her another squeeze, as more photos were snapped by the ever-present Kristen, smiling and taking into account each member of the family and getting shots of each connection. After that it was Jesse and Mel's turn to take them into a group hug. Then Henry shyly hugged Stacie, and Xandy squeezed her hand politely.

Stacie caught glimpses of the friends queuing up to get an opportunity to speak to them, and she saw Sue and Paul looking over the tables at the beautiful flowers Sue had arranged, while waiting their turn. Zack pounded Tyson on the back, and Nina gave him a hug as they congratulated him, while Ava and Andrew, stunning together, matching in black, embraced Stacie. Andrew looked happier than she had seen him in months with Ava on his arm. Out of the corner of her eye she saw Karen Walters smiling at her; Stacie knew soon Karen would be ordering her to sit down. She gave Karen a knowing wink, as if promising to behave herself. When a small guest appeared at her elbow, Stacie looked down to see Allie, pretty in her pink organza dress, tugging on her dress, wanting a hug from the bride. She knelt down after motioning to Kristen to get their picture together and then with Bets and Jim by the beautiful wedding cake. "Where's your veil?" asked Allie, puzzled.

"I didn't want to wear one," Stacie said, wrinkling her nose, and Allie giggled. "You look like a bride yourself!" she told Allie who hid behind Bets' skirt, laughing. "This cake is amazing!" Stacie complimented Bets, noticing how perfectly she had copied the camellias in all the different shades across the cake's round tiers. She knew it would taste as heavenly as it looked. Then Sue appeared and Stacie hugged her, thanking her for all the lovely flowers. Tyson was slipping farther away from her; she caught his eye and he made his sad face across the crowd to her, making her laugh.

Jeanna and Rob were hugging her next, tiny Jeanna always impeccable and lovely with her sleek dark bob and large friendly eyes. "I know I shouldn't tell you this on your wedding day..." Jeanna began after congratulating Stacie, keeping her eye on Tyson across several bodies.

"What is it?" Stacie asked curiously.

"I ran into *Torie* today at Gray's," Jeanna said, wide-eyed, fingering her green, beaded necklace a little nervously.

Stacie gasped and put her hand to her mouth. She looked around for Tyson too. "No! Tell me more! Is she back for good?"

"She said she's just here for the weekend with Ellie. She's planning to hold out as long as she can to see if Rick can really pull this off. So far, she's been impressed. He told her you had helped him put some things in perspective. I didn't know you had talked to him!"

Stacie shook her head, disbelievingly. "Well...I went by the restaurant a while ago, just to see what was going on. I didn't realize he took what I said to heart."

"Evidently you made more of an impact than you thought. Way to go!" Jeanna said, squeezing her arm as Lucy and Terry made their way through the crowd to get their hugs while the priest tapped his glass.

"Don't go anywhere after you cut the cake," Murph warned her suspiciously. "We have a special toast we want to make, so heads up."

"Okay," Stacie agreed conspiratorially. At that moment, the dinner was to be served and Father Jack, with his tiny wife, Leigh, beside him, was ready to administer the blessing.

As Tyson guided Stacie through the buffet line, their parents joked behind them about the wedding ceremony. It had been lost on Stacie that when Father Jack asked Tyson whether he would have her for his lawfully wedded wife he had declared, "*Absolutely!*" to the delight of everyone.

"Oh, honey, how did you miss that?" Elaine laughed, looking at Stacie.

"I don't know! I was just in a trance! I guess I just floated through the whole thing. I didn't want to miss any of it, but I guess I did," Stacie laughed, gazing at her hot husband, who grinned at her and served a slice of roast beef onto her plate.

"You'll be glad you had it videotaped," her father said, his eyes twinkling at her.

Her college roommate, Tina, her husband, and their teenage children appeared at her elbow before they sat down at the table and gave her hugs as she introduced them proudly to Tyson. Even with the distraction of so many people, Stacie felt riveted to Tyson during the meal, with the lively conversation. She looked forward to the evening they would eventually spend together as husband and wife at the little inn her father had arranged for them as their honeymoon. They knew they would not get more than one night of a honeymoon, but it was all she would need with him. She was surprised to feel how this night would be so different from all their other nights together, even in their circumstances, and even at their age, but the commitment they had made to each other had changed everything for her. Tyson was looking at her now, amused, or surprised at her misty eyes; he took her hand under the table, smiling knowingly at her.

After dinner, more toasts were made and more tears flowed down Stacie's cheeks, as the caterers arrived and removed their dishes. It was time for some dancing.

Sugar Fisher was calling out to Stacie and Tyson.

"Would the newlyweds join each other in the center of the room please?" she requested in her raspy, sexy voice as a spotlight illuminated the dance floor where they were meant to stand. As Tyson took Stacie's hand again, Sugar said, "That's more like it! How 'bout a nice Mr. and Mrs. Garrett kiss before we get started?" She laughed and glasses clinked all around them. Tyson raised his eyebrows and nodded, taking Stacie in his arms, dipping her back, and kissing her the way he had done on the altar. There was applause and Sugar was giving them her approval. "Okay…here's a little song for the bride and groom to dance to. This is Tyson's pick, Stacie!" she said and the music started. Everyone recognized the Marvin Gaye song as she began to sing in her sultry voice, "Let's Get It On." Laughter followed and Tyson looked at her dubiously to more laughter from the onlookers.

"Okay…just kidding, Ty. Actually, Stacie picked the song. Here we go!" The music changed and Sugar started belting out in true Aretha Franklin style: "R-E-S-P-E-C-T" and the crowd laughed again.

"Thanks, Sug! I'm glad you have my back!" Stacie called.

"All right, enough fun, now. And by the way, you look really *hot*, Stacie!" Sugar couldn't help but say, and the crowd applauded again. "And you too Tyson! For a white guy, you know? Okay, this is it. We're all so glad you guys are finally married…*at last!*" The music started again, and this time the Etta James classic love song "At Last" pealed forth soulfully from Sugar Fisher's lips.

Tyson wrapped his arm around Stacie's waist and held her hand as they danced in the spotlight. He put his lips close to her ear and murmured to her softly, "So, Mrs. Garrett, you *do* look really hot. I just want to *rip that dress right off you*, right here, right now. I don't care who sees." She smiled sweetly as Kristen took their picture again, and they heard the tinkling sound of people tapping their silverware on their glasses, urging them to kiss once more.

"You're really enjoying yourself, aren't you?" she said, smiling up at him and kissing him tenderly in front of all of their family and friends.

"I am indeed, boss. This is *our* night!" he laughed and tenderly kissed her back, as much for their audience as for himself.

When their dance was over, Sugar called out to the father of the bride and Stacie's father appeared at her elbow for his turn on the dance floor with her. He swept her up in his warm embrace and kissed her on the cheek, "From Mom and me," he whispered as Sugar declared him "hot" as well, which made him laugh heartily as all the ladies applauded. They danced to Sugar's sweet version of "My Girl" by the Temptations, and they did their best attempt at the shag on the dance floor. Then everyone joined them and Tyson was back in her arms again, as Dan had found Elaine for the next song, another slow one.

"I think my brother's in love with you!" Tyson told her as he turned her slowly around the floor, still in the spotlight.

"Jesse? He's such a sweetheart. I'd have gone for him, too, if I didn't know about you, and if he weren't married to Mel," she said coyly.

"Hmm, good to know," he laughed in her ear. "But actually, I was talking about Henry!"

Stacie's eyebrows shot up. She felt immediately uncomfortable and glanced around. Sure enough, Henry was leaning on the bar with the same dreamy expression she'd seen on his face back in the summer, watching her swaying in his brother's arms. "Oh, that's too weird. What about Sandy with an X? Where is she?" They both looked around and found her in a group, drinking champagne, and talking with Ava, Lilia, and Alex, who were back from school for the event.

"Get ready, I think he's going to cut in," Tyson said, and she saw Henry walking toward them. She swallowed and he was there, tapping on Tyson's shoulder.

"Mind if I cut in?" he asked. Stacie stepped aside, gesturing to Tyson.

"Not at all. Y'all have fun," she said and immediately found Karen Walters to embrace, whom she hadn't had a chance to see yet, leaving both men with their mouths hanging open in disbelief. She smiled and winked at Tyson as he shook his head slightly at her, going for a beer with Henry to the bar. There was a commotion by the door with her parents, Shelly, and Tom and Liz. She realized with relief that Kyle and Chelsea had just safely arrived and were being smothered in hugs. She caught Tyson's eye again and they converged on the two, barely in the doorway and looking exhausted. Kyle, in a navy blazer and tie, held tight to Chelsea's hand. Chelsea was a knockout, as usual, slender and elegant in a silver dress with sparkly little stars at her ears.

"Look at you guys! I'm *so* glad you're finally here!" Stacie crooned to them, another tear beginning as the way was being cleared for her to greet these two very important guests. The three of them melted into an embrace, filled with love, laughter, and relief that they were all finally together.

"Hey, Stace! Congratulations! Tears…you?" Kyle said, noticing her radiant though wet cheeks.

"I've cried more since last summer than I have in my whole life! But they've all been good tears. I'm so happy right now!"

"We're so glad to finally be here," he said, taking Tyson by the shoulder. "You guys look great!" he added as Stacie wrapped her arms around Chelsea.

"We lucked out that you didn't have to dance today!" Stacie told her.

"I know, right? It's fall break for us. It was great getting to go to Kyle's game. And they won, too!"

"We heard. Congrats, man!" Tyson said, slapping Kyle on the back.

"You guys must be exhausted!" said Stacie. "Matt and Erin saved dinner for you."

"Great! We haven't eaten," said Kyle. "Chelsea changed in the car after our last pit stop, but otherwise, we drove straight here."

Stacie flashed a look to Sugar Fisher and the band began Kyle's favorite song, Percy Sledge's classic, "When A Man Loves A Woman," and he and Chelsea were nudged out onto the dance floor with the rest of the guests. Kyle winked at Stacie, and she watched him pull Chelsea into his arms, saying "Wow!" into her ear.

"Okay, everything is right with the world right now," Stacie told Tyson and felt herself relax considerably. She dissolved into his arms and felt him rock her back and forth soulfully to the music.

"You need to sit down after this, okay?" he said gently to her.

"Okay, I'll be ready," she said, but at the end of the song, Sugar and Kristen had other ideas. It was time to cut the cake. Sugar talked them through it as Kristen snapped more pictures. Then Stacie watched, puzzled, as Sugar handed the microphone to Murph, and Stacie remembered the heads-up she had given her before. Shelly, Bets, and Sue were crowding around her as well, and Murph was holding an envelope.

"Well, you guys are the best couple we know, but you sure are the hardest to do things for! All of us here tonight were so exasperated that neither of you wanted any gifts that we had to take matters into our own hands." She laughed and motioned to an entourage of people to come up to the stage: Nina, Zack, Andrew, Bobby, Chrystal, and Billy were making their way to the stage, while Murph continued. "We knew you wouldn't believe it, but these kind folks have all agreed to take over the operation of The Sound Side for the next several days so you two can get away. And what finer place to honeymoon than in *Bermuda*!" The guests began to applaud and grin, watching Stacie's jaw drop open in shock. When Tyson reacted the same way, she was happy that he seemed as surprised as she was.

"You'll be flying out on Monday and staying in the resort for five days.

We know your passports are good after that little jaunt the two of you took to the Caymans last Christmas. Bets and Jim will be taking care of Mojo so you're really free! Happy honeymoon, guys, from all of us!" As the applause started up again, Murph handed the microphone back to Sugar and came over to give them the envelope.

"What did you do? I'm so shocked!" Stacie cried, hugging her friend. "You guys are so amazing!"

"This is doctor-approved. We've consulted with Karen about the safest place for you all to go and she supports this, as long as you promise to behave yourself!" Murph laughed.

"I've got that under control," smiled Tyson and squeezed Murph as well. "This is beyond fabulous! We can't thank everyone enough." He beckoned to Sugar and took the microphone from her; then he thanked all the guests for their support, for traveling all the distances they'd come, for their love, and especially for the trip. "We had no idea this could be possible for us. We never would have asked you to do such a generous thing as this. So thank you, everyone, for making this happen. I *promise* I'll take good care of her while we're gone!" He gave a special wink to Dan, and then another meaningful look to Karen. "And now, if you all would please continue having fun, I'm going to ask my beautiful bride to sit down with me for a while!"

They sat at their places at the wedding table while Chelsea and Kyle joined them and dinner plates were brought to them by the catering staff. Stacie covered Chelsea's hand with hers. "I'm so glad you all had a safe trip here. I'm sure you're exhausted!" she said, looking over Kyle for any bumps and bruises. "You look like you're all in one piece!" she laughed as he ate hungrily from his plate.

"Yep, no injuries, just sore all the time," he said, taking a sip from his glass of tea. "I got to play today," he said with a grin.

"Not only did he play but he scored, too! A thirty-yard run for a touchdown," Chelsea bragged, hugging him around the shoulders. "I'm so glad I was there to see it," she said, smiling broadly at him, and taking a bite of green beans. She looked different, more confident, older, and even more gorgeous than ever, if it were possible, thought Stacie, marveling at the two of them…her college kids, she thought, as Shelly, Liz, and Tom were heading toward the table with drinks and wedding cake.

Stacie asked quickly before the conversation got away from them. "And how's dancing?"

Chelsea's smile broadened more. "It's great! I really love it there. It's such a change from what I'm used to, and high school, and I love being challenged. I just really miss this guy," she said and her smile faded just a bit as they held hands at the table, with their matching hemp bracelets.

"It was really good getting caught up on the ride up here," Kyle said, looking at Chelsea admiringly. "It's been way too long," he commented.

More people came and went as Stacie held court from her seat at the table, at times with Allie on her lap. Then it was time to toss the bouquet and fling the garter. Chrystal caught the bouquet, although Stacie had been aiming for a spot between Ava and Nina. Zack snatched the garter out of the air, knocking over a couple of guys from New Jersey in the process, to everyone's amusement.

"We've never left here with this many people in the place before. Don't you feel a little nervous?" Tyson said into Stacie's ear as they prepared to leave.

"It's kind of odd, but I'm trusting Nina and Erin. Nina told me not to worry. It'll be like it never happened when we see the place again…and that will be in about six days. Now, that is weird!" They hugged everyone and made their way to the car, under the traditional rain of birdseed.

After the proprietor of the inn had deposited them and their one bag at the door, Tyson swept Stacie up in his arms and carried her over the threshold of their room. The first thing they noticed was the old squeaky wooden floor and the presence of no other noise, not even the hum of an air conditioning unit anywhere nearby. He continued to hold her in his arms and bounced on the floor a little, listening to the squeak-squeak of the creaky floor. They laughed into each other's faces.

"So, Mrs. Garrett, I guess we'll have to be quiet tonight!" Tyson said, his lips on her face.

"Then you brought the wrong girl, Mr. Garrett," she joked, loosening her hair from its twist as he set her down. "It looks like nobody's on that side of us," she said, inclining her head to the left and sitting on the bed, toeing off her ivory shoes. She stretched out onto her elbow, watching him remove his jacket, folding it across the back of a chair, and untying his tie.

"Maybe we should turn on the TV for some noise…" he suggested, unbuttoning his cuffs, and pulling out his shirttail.

She wrinkled her nose and went to him. "Making love in front of the TV has never been a turn-on for me," she said, taking over the unbuttoning of his shirt.

"Well, then off it stays," he said, laughing at her hungry expression. He noticed the champagne chilling in the ice bucket on the table. "More champagne…."

"Open it if you want it," she smiled.

"It's no fun if you can't have it, too. Besides, I'm done. I just got over my hangover from last night when we got to the church."

"You won't be disappointed if I don't emerge from the bathroom in one of those little lacy negligees, will you?" she asked coyly, slowly pushing away his shirt with the palms of her hands and loosening his belt.

"Nope. It's a waste of time and fabric, if you ask me," he said, pulling off his pants and then his socks.

"I keep telling people that and nobody gets it," she laughed, sliding her hands across the smoothness of his back and shoulders. She pressed her mouth into the side of his neck.

"This, however, was *not* a waste of fabric," he said, slipping his finger inside the ivory silk at the neckline of her dress. "The only problem was, I couldn't wait to get it off of you," he added, expertly unzipping it at the small of her back, giving her a little shiver as his hands slid up her skin. He tugged twice at the tie of her dress and the ivory silk fell around her ankles in an instant. His green eyes burned into her as he watched her remove her panties. He flipped off the light, helping her into the bed with him.

"Any more tears tonight?" he asked her gently, kissing her, stroking his fingers into her hair, and taking her into his warm embrace.

"Oh, I think you can count on it," she said, bursting with love for him, her voice about to break…and then she felt it again, the fluttering inside her. Quickly, she pulled the palm of his hand to the tight, small roundness of her belly, and he felt the movement with her as it happened again. She gasped, watching his reaction.

"Oh, God!" he breathed. She smiled at him, sharing his first moment of awe. He started to speak again and failed, blinking, unable to draw his hand away from her. His face dissolved and tears brimmed over his eyelids as he buried his face in her hair.

Chapter 13

SIX MONTHS LATER

Stacie wandered into the nursery, the full moon shining, beacon-like, through the window. She switched on the little nightlight, a half-moon with an angel curled up asleep in its curve. Stretching, she sat on the futon and pushed back into the pillows to attempt to get comfortable. Getting comfortable had been harder to do in the last few days. They did not know whether the baby was a boy or a girl, but they did know that it was stuck in a breech presentation, which made for some discomfort on Stacie's part. Its head pushed hard against the top of her ribcage. It was stretching out, too, at the moment. Mojo jumped up onto the futon and plodded around in circles, trying to find just the right place to settle, watching Stacie's face as she rolled sideways, sighing. After rubbing her cat's soft head, Stacie lifted her soft loose shirt and watched the baby's head as it moved from side to side, contorting her large stomach like a lava lamp.

"Are you trying to turn?" she asked the child inside her, stroking it with her hands as if she could soothe it. She gazed at the crib, covered in a patchwork quilt and matching bumper pads her mother and Shelly had found for her shower. She smiled slightly at the framed poster of the cover of one of her favorite books, *Where the Wild Things Are* by Maurice Sendak. She knew that, boy or girl, their child would have her penchant for excitement and her energy. Her energy had worn her parents out in her childhood, but had been a Godsend in her chosen career. She could never have existed, sitting behind a desk or doing the most meticulous tasks, but give her a restaurant to run and multiple tasks all day long, and she was in heaven! She liked crowds and action; wildness ran in her veins as sure as her blood.

It was a Friday night, March 17th, St. Patrick's Day, one of her favorite party days of the year, and here she was, stretched out on the couch at home and it wasn't even ten o'clock yet! The college people were all in for their spring break, and Bangelic was probably starting in on its Celtic set at this moment. She wished she were there. Being a mother was going to take some getting used to, but she knew she could do it. She wanted to do it. She knew there were things she would miss, but she had stopped caring. She smiled again, gazing at the little collection of clothing she had folded earlier in the day, a white hooded sweater, and little yellow and green outfits that would be appropriate for a boy or a girl. Bets had given her a collection of white, yellow, and green bows, in case she had a girl, so everyone would know. Her friends…they never seemed to understand her…not wanting wedding presents, no fancy lingerie, not wanting to know the baby's sex. She and Tyson had been in agreement on that, too. They just hoped and prayed that whoever it was would make it to term and would be healthy. Wanting to know the gender seemed like too much to ask. Plus, it was so much fun wagering with Tyson! He was sure it was a girl, but she knew it was a boy. There was a betting pool going on right now at the St. Paddy's Day party at The Sound Side. It was almost as much fun as betting on the basketball tournament she was sure they were all watching over there.

At that moment, the baby's head moved back to the other side, and she watched in amazement as it happened in her body. Even Mojo seemed to know something was up and looked at her with his huge blue eyes as he pricked up his brown ears. She sighed again and tried to relax. The weight room had turned out to be the perfect place for the nursery. Jim Brantley had gladly agreed to take the exercise equipment off their hands, although Bets was not fond of losing her garage space for the gym conversion. The room had more space than Stacie remembered, and it still allowed them to have a guest room, which would come in handy since her mother had promised to come and stay for short visits to help them out. She also had college girls clamoring for opportunities to nanny for her over the summer, which was a nice surprise.

They were ready, as ready as they'd ever be. The C-section was scheduled for Monday morning. The plan had been due in part to Stacie's risk with the fibroid tumors, and now, partially due to the baby's breech position. Stacie massaged her belly, wishing Tyson would get on home, as this was usually his job. His massage, or maybe it was the depth and resonance of his voice, seemed to calm the baby so it would go to sleep and then she could rest as well. It wouldn't be long before he would be walking through the door. It was probably harder for him to get away tonight with everyone there. Henry had shown up to their surprise as well. He still had the thing going on with Xandy, who was also in from Carolina with her parents at their beach house. Tyson and Henry had almost become close, following their visit to charming Cape May in January, before Henry headed back to New York for his last semester of law school. It had been her last trip anywhere before the baby's birth, and it had been wonderful to say the least. She felt as if she were truly part of Tyson's family now, and his parents and siblings were glad to have Tyson back in the fold as well. Connie and Wade called every other day to check on them, just as her own parents did. Shelly was beside herself with the anticipation of becoming an aunt, and Stacie was glad she had her job and her own friends now as a diversion.

She felt a kick near her pubic bone, then two more in succession, and felt a pop, as if a champagne cork were going off inside her! Warm water gushed between her legs and she sprang off the futon, grabbing her cell phone and running for the bathroom. She snatched a towel off the rack and pushed her pants down around her ankles, pulling them off and tossing them into a pile on the floor as she sat on the toilet and tried to collect herself. Mojo stood at the doorway of the bathroom, staring at her with wide blue eyes, and yowling. Her hands shook as she reached for her phone and pushed the speed dial button for Tyson. He answered on the third ring.

"Hey!" he said jovially; she could hear music and people in the background. "You'll never guess what just happened!" he laughed into the phone, and she laughed ironically as well.

"Okay, you go first," she said, feeling the drip slowing a bit between her legs.

"Zack just proposed to Nina!" he laughed again, and she felt some of the tension melt away.

"Ohh! That's great!"

"What? Hold on…I can hardly hear you," he said, and she knew he was walking outside where he could hear away from the music and commotion. "Okay, this is better. Isn't that great?" he asked. She could tell he was excited and nowhere near ready to leave.

"Yeah, it's awesome. Tell them I said congratulations. Listen, I need you to come on home. My water just broke!"

"*What?*" he shouted into the phone. "When? Where are you? Are you okay?"

"Yeah. I'm sitting on the toilet. I was sitting on the futon in the baby's room and it just happened, like a champagne cork popping. This baby's ready to get here."

"Holy *crap*! Okay, I'm leaving, right now! I'll be there in ten minutes. Did you call Karen?"

"No, but she's the next call I make. Drive safely, okay?"

It took seven rings for the answering service to connect and tell her that Dr. Walters was already at the hospital. The person with whom Stacie spoke told her she would have Karen paged and that she would call her as soon as she was available. She sat on the toilet with her head in her hands, feeling giddy and surreal. She worried there would be a stain on the nice new yellow futon cover, but she was still leaking fluid and did not trust herself to get up and walk around. She was alone. What if she passed out? That wouldn't be good for the baby or her. As she was beginning to talk herself into getting up, her phone rang again. It was a frustrated Tyson on the other end.

"My fucking truck won't start!" he growled into the phone, and then he laughed. "But I've got a boatload of volunteers who want to drive me over and get you!"

"Like who?"

He seemed to cover his mouth and his response was muffled, "Well, Father Jack, for one, but I'm opting for Henry right now. Kyle just left."

Stacie rolled her eyes and wailed into the phone. "Oh, no! Henry's not with Sandy with an X, is he?" She was imagining Xandy's displeasure at having her car seats spoiled by her leaking amniotic fluid.

"Well, she can drop me at the house and then I'll drive us over in your car. You won't even have to see them."

"Thank you, love of my life!" she sighed, relieved into the phone. "Karen's already at the hospital, so we'll just head right over there, I guess. Here she is, beeping in now."

"Okay. I'm coming in ten minutes. Bye, baby!"

Stacie switched over to the other number beeping in. "This is Karen. What's happening, Stacie?"

"Hey! My water just broke and I'm sitting on the toilet, waiting for Tyson to get here."

"Are you having any contractions yet?"

"I don't think so."

"Good. Come on over here and get checked in. I'm getting ready to do a C-section right now. It'll take forty-five minutes, so I'll see you then. We'll go ahead and do yours next. No sense in waiting till Monday, since you've got a breech presentation going on. Dang full moon does this every time! Who knew there were this many babies coming on the island!"

"All right. I'll see you in forty-five."

"Tell Tyson to take deep breaths and watch his driving! He'll be more of a wreck than you are. See you!"

Stacie sighed, watching Mojo pace the bathroom doorway, yowling at her from time to time. "It's okay, sweetie," she murmured, sitting up straight to give the baby enough room. She was getting tired of this position and just wanted to lie down in her bed. It didn't help that she felt tired. She was going to have a long few hours ahead of her...and then she would *never sleep again*!

She heard an engine slow and a car roll into her driveway. A door slammed and quick footsteps raced up the stairs of the beach house. She heard the door open, and Tyson was kneeling beside her in no time. He looked so delighted that she had to smile. "Hey!" he said, taking her hand and placing the palm of his other hand on her stomach. She stroked his hair. "Did you talk to Karen?" he asked, looking at her, gauging the situation.

"Yes. She said to come on over and drive slow! She wants to go ahead with this tonight."

He was on his feet, rubbing his hands on his jeans, pushing up the sleeves of his fleece pullover. "Okay…your bag," he said, pointing toward the bedroom. They heard Henry's voice calling Tyson's name.

"*Shit!*" screeched Stacie. "*What is he doing here?* I thought they dropped you off?"

"They did," he said, taking a step back, puzzled, as Henry's head appeared in the doorway and Stacie's jaw dropped open.

"Oh, crap! Sorry! Hey, Stacie. Dude, you left your phone in the car," Henry said, trying not to look at Stacie, who had nowhere to hide. "Okay, I'm outta here. Good luck, guys!" His voice carried from the stairway and they heard his feet trip-trapping down the stairs.

She rolled her eyes and looked at Tyson. He laughed anxiously, pocketing his phone, and went into the bedroom to get her bag that had been packed and ready for a week. She began barking out orders from her toilet. "Do you mind pulling that futon cover off and sticking it in the washing machine?"

"Sure!" he said. She heard him in the nursery and the sound of cloth being pulled away from the mattress. She saw him walk by the door and said, "And squirt some stuff on it before you put it in the washer."

"Okay." She heard squirting. "What setting do you want it on?" She heard his animated voice from down the hall. He was in high gear.

"Cold…*please*," she threw in, laughing. She wondered whether anything else needed to be done. Nothing was in the oven at this hour and the back door was locked, or should have been. "Will you check the back door to see if it's locked?" she said as soon as his face was in the doorway. He was back in two seconds, picking up her clothes off the floor and adding them to the washing machine.

"What do you think is wrong with the truck?" she asked absently, listening to the water come on and then the sound of him pouring dry food into Mojo's bowl and running tap water from the sink into his water bowl. She heard him washing his hands at the kitchen sink.

"Probably just a dead battery," he responded just as absently. He was back in the bathroom with her.

"So, what are you wearing to this party?" he asked, hands on his hips, trying to humor her; she felt a little rush of love for him.

"A swimsuit would be appropriate!" she said, smiling broadly. "Maybe that pair of black stretch pants…and another pair of underwear, please," she requested as he ducked out of the doorway once again. She wrapped the towel around her and went to the cabinet under the sink in search of a large pad, the kind she loathed wearing, but which would come in handy in just a moment. He was back with the clothes.

"Want some help?"

"No, thanks. I've got it. This could get ugly…" she warned him and he stepped out of the door.

When she was dressed, he helped her into her jacket and took her bag. They said goodbye to Mojo and headed out the door. Tyson held her elbow as they went downstairs slowly and got into her car. "Jeez, just look at that moon!" he said as he installed her carefully into her seat and placed her bag in the backseat. "This is it!" he said, grinning, and he kissed her before taking his spot in the driver's seat.

Abigail Edmonds Garrett was born at 11:57 p.m. on St. Patrick's Day. She weighed seven pounds and five ounces and was "as healthy as a horse," according to Dr. Karen. On Saturday morning, Tyson walked back into the hospital room after sneaking away to the coffee shop to grab a much needed cup of coffee. He sat beside Stacie on the bed as she held Abigail to her breast. "Look at you guys! Alone, at last," he said, referring to the hustle and bustle of the morning, with nurses coming in and out to check on Stacie, to bring breakfast, and then to bring Abigail in to have her first taste of mother's milk. The lactation specialist had just left. Stacie smiled up at him, exhausted as they both were. Sleeping in a hospital was an oxymoron, as far as she could tell.

He watched their little girl suck vigorously at Stacie's breast, her tiny hands still in fists at her face from her confinement, bright eyes looking around. "It took her a while to settle down. She woke up really hungry, they said. I guess you're going to have to share," she said as he watched with interest.

"I'm cool with that," he said. "Does it hurt?"

"Not really. You did a nice job of preparing me for this."

"My pleasure. Look at her. She's perfect!" he said in wonder. "I hate to tell you this, but there's a crowd of people planning to be here today. If you're not up for it…I'll try to keep them at bay."

"Oh, I know they'll all want to see her. We'll play it by ear."

"How are you feeling? In much pain?"

"Some. I guess more than usual from having the tumors removed after she was born." She glanced over at the IV stand with the morphine drip. She had thought twice about using it, but the nurses had said it wouldn't hurt the baby. The drug made her ears roar and she didn't want any part of it, but it did seem to manage the pain.

"Do you remember all of it?"

"Oh, yeah! I might have missed the whole wedding, but I wasn't planning on missing this! Even when they gave me the gas for the nausea, I felt a little stoned, but I tried to hang on for every bit of it. I remember you taking her out to show Shelly and Kyle and Chelsea. I could hear you all talking and how excited you all were."

"Your parents are on their way, and Father Jack's going to come over here and give her a blessing," he said, sipping his coffee.

"That will be really special," she said happily as he smiled at her. Then she looked at him and said softly, "We did it!"

"Yeah, we did. Did you doubt it?"

"Did you?"

"Like I said, second time's a charm."

"Well, you were right. You've been right about a lot of things."

"I love it when you say that," he smiled at her. "And now, let's discuss that wager we had. Seems I was right about that, too."

"We never set the terms. So, what do you want?"

He thought a minute. "You've given me half the restaurant and half the house. Let's see; I still get sex, right?"

"We'll see about that. It might not be up to me," she said. They gazed at little fair-haired Abigail, who had fallen asleep during her breakfast. Stacie looked questioningly at him and he put down his coffee cup, taking his daughter from her arms, and kissed her tiny forehead.

"Well…I can't think of anything else. I *know* you don't have any money," he said, his green eyes crinkling and his dimples forming. "I guess I've gotten everything I've ever wanted, then."

She placed her hand under his arms, under their child, and he leaned in to kiss her.

"I'd say all *three* of us won this bet!" she said happily.

A Forever Man - Book Four

"There are friends and there are lovers; sometimes the line between is thinly drawn."

"Just when I thought I would never see Kyle and Chelsea Davis again, Mary Flinn brings them back in *A Forever Man*; they returned like old friends you feel comfortable with no matter how much time has passed, only this time with eight-year-old twin boys, and a new set of life-complications to work through. In this novel, Flinn provides a deft look at marriage when potential infidelity threatens it. *A Forever Man* is Flinn's masterpiece to date, and no reader will be disappointed."

~Tyler R. Tichelaar, Ph.D., award-winning author of *Spirit of the North: a paranormal romance* and *The Best Place*

INTRODUCING A NEW, STAND-ALONE NOVEL, APART FROM THE KYLE AND CHELSEA SERIES, THE NEST...

"Mary Flinn realistically captures the ideals of an empty nest filled with rekindling passions of soon-to-retire Cherie and her rock-and-roll-loving husband Dave—then flips it all over when Hope, the jilted daughter, returns to the nest to heal her broken heart. Between her mother's comical hot flashes that only women of a certain age could appreciate, the loss of her laid-back father's sales job, and the good news-bad news of other family members' lives, can Hope find the courage to spread her wings and leave the nest again? Flinn's deft handling of story-telling through both Cherie and Hope's voices will send readers on a tremendously satisfying and wild flight back to *The Nest*."

~Laura S. Wharton, author of the award-winning novels *Leaving Lukens, The Pirate's Bastard,* and others

About the Author

A native of North Carolina, award-winning author Mary Flinn long ago fell in love with her state's mountains and its coast, creating the backdrops for her series of novels, *The One*, *Second Time's a Charm*, *Three Gifts*, and *A Forever Man*. With degrees from both the University of North Carolina at Greensboro and East Carolina University, Flinn has retired from her first career as a speech pathologist in the NC public schools that began in 1981. Writing a novel had always been a dream for Flinn, who began crafting the pages of *The One*, when her younger daughter left for college at Appalachian State University in 2009. The characters in this book continued to call to her, wanting more of their story told, which bred the next three books in the series.

Flinn has recently been the recipient of the Reader Views Literary Awards 2012 Reviewers' Choice honorable mention in the romance category for *A Forever Man*. First Place Award for Romance Novel in the Reader Views 2011 Literary Book Awards, as well as the Pacific Book Review Best Romance Novel of 2011 went to *Three Gifts*. *Second Time's a Charm*, also released in 2011, won an Honorable Mention in the Reader Views Literary Awards.

Mary Flinn lives in Summerfield, North Carolina with her husband, and near her two adult daughters.

The Nest is her fifth novel.

www.TheOneNovel.com